ANNA/BELLA

Also by
AMANDA SWIFT

THE BOYS' CLUB

BIG BONES

ANNA / BELLA

AMANDA SWIFT

SIMON AND SCHUSTER

SIMON AND SCHUSTER
First published in Great Britain by Simon & Schuster UK Ltd, 2006
A CBS COMPANY

5 7 9 10 8 6 4

Simon & Schuster UK Ltd
Africa House
64–78 Kingsway
London WC2B 6AH

A CIP catalogue record for this book is available from the British Library

ISBN-10: 1-4169-0473-5
ISBN-13: 978-1-4169-0473-1

Typeset by Rowland Phototypesetting Ltd, Bury St Edmunds, Suffolk
Printed and bound in Great Britain by Cox & Wyman Ltd, Reading, Berkshire

For Godfrey

ONE

Ever wondered what it's like to be two people at once? Well, to be more accurate, one person for half the week and someone else for the other. That's me – Anna/Bella. Anna at Mum's, Bella at Dad's. Anna likes baked potatoes, *Blue Peter* and books about wars, bullying or homelessness. Bella likes sushi, MTV and any book with a shiny cover. I know it sounds mad but I can't seem to stop it now I've started.

It all began about six months ago, when I went to secondary school, in September last year. Mum and Dad chose that stressful time to heap even more stress on me: they finally split up. Maybe they thought it would be good to make a clean break but it was so stressful it broke me in two.

I don't blame them for splitting up, though. They've never got on, not as far back as I can remember. They claim they used to hold hands and do all that soppy stuff when they first met but once I was born they were at loggerheads. I can't work out if it was my fault for being born or their fault for not getting on. Neither way is great for me and my self-confidence; no wonder I've turned out so weird.

Although I can't deny that being two people actually suits me. I was always Anna while we all lived together; I became Bella, too, when Dad moved out and I started to stay with him. I decided that the new me would have a new name and I chose Bella because my real name is Annabella, but no one ever calls me that.

So Anna is the old me, the primary school me. When I'm Anna, I wear cheap old clothes and I don't care much what I look

2

like. I'm not into boys in a big way and I spend lots of time sewing and making things with my best friend Eve.

Bella is the new me, the secondary school me. I was so scared of going to secondary school, especially as it wasn't the same school as Eve's. When we went to look round the school all the girls looked so mature and sophisticated I realised I would have to grow up fast to catch up with them. So when I went to Dad's I did it suddenly and in one go instead of doing it slowly and bit by bit.

When I first went to stay at Dad's he gave me an allowance. That's how it all began. I went out and bought lots of clothes and for the first time ever I could buy what I wanted. I bought all the stuff Mum disapproves of: tight little tops, designer jeans, high heels. I bought make-up and hair slides and fancy handbags. Mum never wanted me to buy anything like that but Dad didn't notice. He's always so busy working that he'd only notice what I was wearing if I went and sat on his desk.

Even though I wanted to change and get new gear, I didn't want to upset Mum by wearing it when I was with her, so I decided to wear my new clothes at Dad's and my old clothes at Mum's. Then I got a bit cheeky. I pretended to Dad that Mum didn't get me any new clothes (which is sort of true because she gets everything from boot sales) so I had to have a big allowance to pay for clothes to wear at Mum's house.

That's how this stupid habit of changing clothes between houses started, but it's not easy. Take today, for example. It's Saturday, I started the day at Dad's and at about 11.08 I set off for Mum's. I usually leave at 11.00 but I got to Dad's eight minutes late yesterday due to the bus being late, so I thought I'd give Dad eight extra minutes of my sunny personality this morning. Fact is he was working so we weren't exactly spending quality time together. Still, it was an option if he took a break. He didn't, of course.

'Off to Mum's, Bella?' he asked, as he always does, and I always reply:

'Yup.' He knows not to ask any more questions. I know not to give him any more answers. It's easier that way. When they first split up he used to ask me how I was getting there, what I was doing when I got there, what I'd be eating, what I'd be drinking and what I'd be smelling. I'm not kidding, he doesn't like the smell of Mum's incense. He didn't like any of the answers so now he doesn't ask any of the questions.

I set off to the Shopping Centre because I was wearing a tight pink t-shirt with a sequined 'BABE' logo, cut-off jeans, strappy sandals and huge earrings. There was no way I was going to arrive at Mum's looking like that: she'd go nuts. So I'd stuffed a boot-sale denim skirt, old flat suede boots, stripy t-shirt and long floppy cardigan in my bag and headed for the Women's Toilets in the Shopping Centre. Unfortunately there was a queue; even more unfortunately, Jenny from school joined it. Of course I was pleased to see her because she's my joint best friend, but it was bad news because now I wouldn't be able to change.

'Bella!' she shrieked. Jenny's very loud and enthusiastic. 'What are you doing here?'

'Same as you,' I fibbed, because I don't think she'd come to the loo to totally change her clothes and image. Then I leant towards her and whispered: 'But if someone doesn't come out soon I'll be doing it on the floor.'

Jenny snorted with laughter which made me laugh too. 'I mean what are you doing in the Centre, not in the loo.'

'Just window-shopping,' I fibbed again. I really, really hate fibbing and I avoid it whenever I can but with my lifestyle sometimes I have to. Anyway, it wasn't too much of a fib. I'm 12 and a girl so I'm often window-shopping.

'Why do you want to buy a window?' joked Jenny. That's one of our little jokes so I didn't fall about laughing, I just acknowledged it with a grin. I've only known Jenny for six months. We met when I went to secondary school and immediately hit it off.

'What are you looking for?' I asked.

'Apart from a cool boyfriend and straighter hair?'

'Yes,' I said patiently.

'*A Bug's Life* on DVD. I want to copy the American accent so I can be brilliant for the Spotlight audition.' Spotlight's the drama club we go to. Jenny introduced me to it, along with lip gloss. Both have changed my life when I'm Bella. I love lip gloss because it makes me feel older and more alive, like I'm in colour instead of black and white – and so does Spotlight – it's the highlight of my week. It's held in a run-down old church hall and it's led by a drama teacher called Rich.

Anna, the other me, doesn't like lip gloss or drama clubs. She prefers to look natural; but if looking natural means looking pale and spotty, Bella thinks make-up's a must. Anna doesn't like drama clubs because she doesn't like doing anything that involves standing up and shouting while people stare at you, which is why she spends most of her time sitting quietly sewing.

'Can I borrow *A Bug's Life* so I can try to be brilliant too?' I asked Jenny.

'Totally,' she said as I went into the loo at last. I stood there, wondering what to do. I couldn't change now, because I didn't want Jenny to see the tatty old clothes Anna wears. I hung about for a bit, and then heard Jenny in the cubicle next to me.

'I'm praying we both get picked.'

'Praying on the loo? That can't be easy,' I said.

'You know what I mean,' she said.

I did know what she meant. She meant she hoped both of us would be picked for the Spotlight Summer Show. Most of the time at Spotlight we do warm-ups and acting exercises and scenes from plays, but we're just about to start working on our big summer show. It takes weeks to rehearse and then we put the show on for two nights in front of an audience consisting mainly of our embarrassingly enthusiastic parents.

Thinking about the show made me

excited. I love changing my voice, my appearance and my behaviour, especially when I'm *supposed* to be changing them, like at Spotlight, instead of when I'm not supposed to be changing them, like in the rest of my life. At least at Spotlight I get praise for my acting skills; when I'm acting Anna or Bella I just get guilty.

I'd love to tell Jenny all about Anna, but I just don't think she'd like Anna and that would mean she doesn't like me, although she likes me as Bella and that's me too. Oh, it's all so confusing. I wish I could talk to someone about it but there's nobody who knows *both* Anna and Bella, and of course that's exactly the problem I need to talk about. I end up talking to myself, and that's a pretty lonely thing to do, even when there's two of you.

We were just about to go our different ways when Jenny suddenly stared at me wide-eyed, as if I'd just said I didn't like shopping.

'Look left!' she mouthed. I looked to my

left. 'Don't look like you're looking left!' she whispered. I looked to my right. 'He's on your left!' she hissed. I knew by now she must mean Remi. He's the hottest boy in our school football team. He's got a great left foot and fantastic curly hair. His foot doesn't look that good; it's just great at football. His hair doesn't really do anything but flop about. That's enough for me. Remi was walking towards the sports shop with Marcus slouching alongside him.

Marcus is one of those boys who wear his trousers round his knees with designer underpants on show. I think he looks like he needs a belt but Jenny thinks he looks perfect. 'Wow!' she whispered.

'Double wow,' I whispered back. The boys didn't see us, thank goodness, because we were standing staring with our mouths open and almost dribbling (not the footie kind).

After the excitement of the boys walking past I said goodbye to Jenny and then a terrible thing happened. Jenny noticed a tissue. Not a tissue on the floor, or falling out of my bag, or my pocket, or my sleeve, but a tissue falling out of my SHIRT.

'Hey Bella,' she squawked, 'there's a tissue falling out of your shirt!'

'Oh!' I said, as I slapped my hand onto my chest to catch the tissue. I did this as vigorously as if I was swotting a deadly wasp. I nearly fell over with the force of my own hand upon my chest. 'Ha, ha, ha!' I laughed loudly, praying that my embarrassment wouldn't show in my face, because it was certainly showing in the pints of perspiration flowing down my back. 'That's the only place I've got to keep it!' and I very deliberately stuffed the tissue back down my bra.

Jenny looked at me a bit strangely; I'm not surprised. The story was so near the truth I could hardly believe she hadn't guessed it. The fact is that Anna isn't really as 'developed' as Bella. She's only a 32A. Now Jenny is one of those girls who's been looking like a 20-year-old since the age of nine. She's all curves and bumps, all in the right places.

Even before I went to secondary school I was worried about being small. The night before the first day, when my nerves were particularly frayed, I had a long hard look at myself in the mirror. Then, without actually making a decision, I found myself reaching for the box of tissues by my bed. I got a few and made them into a soft cup shape, and stuffed them down my bra. I was pleased with the effect, and did it on the other side. I was thrilled with the result: at least a 32C.

Next day, when I was getting ready for school, I plumped myself up with the tissues again. Once I'd started this trick of course I couldn't stop. Bella had boobs on day one, so she had to have them every day.

Jenny gave me another funny little look but then smiled. Luckily it was true that I didn't have any other pockets so she must have been tempted to believe me.

'You coming to find *A Bug's Life*?' she asked.

'I'd love to but I can't. Got to get off to Mum's.'

'I'll bring it to school on Monday.'

'Cool, dude.'

'Chill, sorted.'

We always say that instead of goodbye. Then we do a high five. Anna doesn't know what a high five is, let alone how to do one, but Bella does them all the time, even with the lollipop lady.

Once Jenny had gone off to the shops I doubled back to the loos again, but as I approached I saw that the queue had tripled in length and what's more, another girl from school was in it. She wasn't a close friend but I didn't want to risk her seeing me change, so I headed out of the Centre and off to Mum's.

TWO

As I walked I racked my brains to think of a place to change. I took a different route from usual, in the vain hope that a change of scene would give me inspiration. Amazingly, inspiration did come, as well as a place to change.

I took a turning down a narrow side-street because I saw some fairy lights twinkling and flashing. When I got closer I saw that they were hung around the window of a clothes shop, but there weren't just clothes in the window. There were plants; and flowers; and a little dog, asleep on a shiny cushion.

I decided to take a closer look. As I

opened the door a tinkling bell rang and a woman's voice called out: 'Hi there!'

I looked around but there was no one in the shop. At the back, there was a doorway with a red velvet curtain hanging where there would normally be a door. The curtain was tied back half-way up, like a curtain in an old-fashioned theatre. I didn't know whether to say anything back, but by then I'd left it too late for it to sound natural, so I didn't say anything.

I looked round the shop. It was stuffed with second-hand clothes, the kind my mum and Anna like. The clothes were arranged on rails, according to colour and these were arranged according to the colours of the rainbow. All in all, it was about as far away from a shopping centre kind of shop as you can get, and it was so different I just stood there looking round and taking it all in.

That's when I saw the screen, standing in the corner with a few dresses hanging from it. It was embroidered with pictures of

Japanese mountains and I could see that the little area behind it was the shop's changing room.

I clutched my bag because I immediately knew how this funny changing room could help me. I moved across the room and slipped through the gap between the screen and the wall. Behind the screen there were two mirrors and a grey cat, asleep on a grey cushion, almost camouflaged. I quickly got out of my sophisticated gear and got into my little girl gear. A brief check in the mirror and I was done. I stuffed the outfit I'd taken off into my bag and made for the door. There was still no one in the shop so I didn't say goodbye, but as I opened the door, the bell rang again.

'Bye,' the same voice called from the back. I was already half-way out of the door and it felt silly saying anything, so I just let the door fall shut and set off down the street. The dog in the window opened an eye and looked at me as I passed.

*

When I got to Mum's I went up to have a read on the bed. Bella hardly ever reads but Anna reads all the time. Lying on my bed reading is one of my favourite things to do at Mum's. Of course I get totally involved in the book and its story, but at the same time I'm aware of myself lying there, reading. The stories I read are far more exciting that anything that happens in my life at the moment, but I don't mind that. I can imagine exciting things happening in the future and I don't mind that they haven't happened yet. I'm quite happy, safe and secure in my little room with its checked curtains and heart-covered bedspread, waiting for my adult life to begin – and trying not to think about the fact that as far as Bella is concerned it already has.

'Anna,' Mum called up the stairs, 'cholesterol's ready!' I was already aware of the delicious smell of bacon wafting up the stairs, so I slid off the bed and followed my nose.

I didn't really need to follow my nose

because I knew dinner would be in the kitchen. Mum was sliding a fried egg onto a plate of bacon and beans. I made piles out of the papers, pens, postcards, key-rings, money and scraps of material on the table. This is one of the only bits of tidying I do at Mum's and it's not because it's on a chore chart like at Dad's, it's because it's the only way I can find any room to eat.

'Any plans?' asked Mum as she fitted my plate into the plate-shaped space I'd managed to make on the table.

'Not really – you?' I answered as I made that delicious first cut into the egg yolk.

'Not really,' answered Mum, and took an enormous gulp of milky coffee. This vague little exchange is a bit of a joke between Mum and me, because it's what we always say on a Saturday. Mum never makes plans; she doesn't plan her day, her week, or her life. She once woke up and decided she wanted to live in Scotland: she was on a train there that afternoon. Admittedly she came back a week later, but she didn't plan that either. Dad, on the other hand, plans everything, even when he's going to floss his teeth.

I hadn't even finished my dinner when the doorbell rang. I was pretty sure it was Eve, because she comes round nearly every Saturday afternoon. As I went to the front door I checked that all the tissues were out of my bra and then I stood still for a moment and put my hands on my hips, in order to stop them wiggling. Bella wiggles so much she looks like she's dislocated at least one hip, but Anna walks as if she's never heard of puberty, let alone lived through it.

'Hi, dude,' I said without thinking.

'Are you feeling all right?' asked Eve, with a little frown on her otherwise smooth, milky white forehead.

'Yeah, sorry,' I said, while I mentally slapped myself. I'd got my hips and my boobs right, but forgotten to remind my tongue I was Anna now. 'Just been watching some teen thing on telly,' I fibbed to cover my mistake. 'Well, only while I was flicking channels.'

'I hate those programmes,' said Eve as she walked in, 'cos there's no horses in them and everyone's always pregnant.'

'Yeah, right,' I said, 'that's why I flicked.'

'What d'you think?' she asked as she held up a square of material in front of her face.

'Nice,' I replied, 'but what is it? A scarf?'

'A skirt, of course.' She dropped it down from in front of her face and thrust it at me for closer scrutiny. 'Want to make one?' she asked as she hopped over the threshold and hung her duffle coat up on top of all the other coats on the one peg in the hall.

'OK, but I'm only here until—'

'I know, I know, you're always only "here until". We can finish it next time you're "here until".'

Eve treats my house a bit like it's her own, which it more or less is because she probably spends as much time at mine as at hers – when I'm there, of course – although she has been known to pop round and see my mum even when I'm at my dad's.

'Hi Eve,' said Mum from behind *Popular*

Patchwork, as Eve came into the kitchen and cleared the junk off a chair so that she could sit down.

'We could get this done this afternoon,' said Eve, reaching into her bag to get out the bits of material she'd brought with her. Mum must have smelled the cotton because she looked up from her mag and scrutinised the skirt.

'Very nice,' she said, smiling, 'and it'd be even nicer with a patchwork jacket.'

'*No*, Mum,' I winced. Mum is mad on patchwork and she makes the most disgusting handbags, waistcoats and tie-dye tablemats. The house is full of fabrics she's going to use 'one day' and Mum is always covered in bits of cotton and thread. It's too much even for Anna, and I have to brush her down before I'll go out with her.

Eve started sorting through the materials she'd brought with her, handing ones she thought I'd like over to me. She was right every time; that's because she is my other joint best friend.

We settled down to make the skirts. We didn't talk much because we were so contented in our making. We've been making things for as long as I can remember: doll's houses out of shoe boxes, hats out of paper, mirrors out of shells, and now real clothes which we actually wear. We've both learnt to sew from our mums and they started teaching us while we were still at nursery.

I've managed to keep my friendship with Eve through all the changes with my parents, my homes, and with me. She's probably the person I'm most sure of and comfortable with in my whole life. I wouldn't do anything to hurt her, especially as she's so tiny and vulnerable. She has a pale face, freckles and a little turned-up nose. Her legs are stick thin and she has the most delicate hands with immaculate, translucent nails.

They're short and unvarnished; so different from Jenny's nails which are long and usually covered in glossy stickers. They'd hate each other's nails; in fact they'd probably hate everything about each other. So how come each half of me likes one of them? What does that say about me, apart from the fact I'm weird?

We hadn't been sewing long when there was another ring at the door. Actually, it was a series of rings, so I knew it was Olly. Olly is Anna's boyfriend and I knew it was him because he's mad on soldiers and battles and he does a ring a bit like morse code. I got up, went into the hall, and checked my hips weren't wiggling before I answered the door.

'Hi,' said Olly with a floppy wave, as if he hadn't really waved at all. He did one of his half smiles which are really cute but he doesn't realise it. He actually does them because he's got a gap in his teeth he's embarrassed of and if he only half smiles it doesn't show.

'Hi,' I said back and did the floppy wave to tease him. He did another half smile and took a step forward. He smelled of Lynx after-shave which he's only just discovered and over-uses. He doesn't actually shave, but his auntie gave him a Lynx deodorant and after-shave set for Christmas so he uses them both all the time because he thinks it would be rude to her not to use them. I don't see why because she lives in Dublin so she's not going to be able to smell it from there. Although with the amount he uses, she probably can.

'Eve's here,' I said quickly so he wouldn't do anything embarrassing like tickle me until I'm giggling hysterically. Instead he leant towards me and gave me the sweetest kiss on the cheek.

'Coming up the park?' he asked, like he always does.

'Eve and I are sewing.'

'OK.'

'Maybe later?'

'Maybe.'

We've been having this kind of conversation for a while now. The fact is that Anna doesn't feel ready to snog anyone, even someone I like as much as Olly, so I always make excuses not to go up to the park because of course snogging is what you do at the park. I don't know how long I'm going to be able to get away with avoiding snogging Olly because he's hairier every time I see him (knees and toes mainly: I've noticed when he wears shorts) so he must be hormonal and that means you want to snog or even 'go further' as Eve puts it. So far my evasion tactics have worked pretty well. In fact the only time we've ever kissed on the mouth was at the Year 6 school disco and even then it was very dark and I've got my suspicions it was someone else.

Olly went to primary school with me and Eve; he was in our class, and when everyone started all that silly 'Who's your boyfriend?' stuff, when we were too young even to know what a boyfriend really was, Olly and I decided we were going out. We didn't actually discuss it, and we certainly didn't do any going out, but Eve said he liked me and I told Eve I liked him and then she told everyone we were an item.

'I'll be off then,' he said, sounding disappointed.

'OK,' I said, sounding relieved.

Olly never says more than he needs to, because he's always trying to save time to get on with his soldiers. He is collecting a huge army and he's worked out it's going to take him eight years to paint it, and that's all day, every day, every weekend. I'm surprised he wants to take time off for snogging, but maybe he's got a bit of a split personality as well: pre-teen Olly who only wants to paint, and teenage Olly who only wants to snog.

Once Olly had gone Eve and I carried on sewing. I found myself wondering what to do about Olly. I can't avoid snogging him for ever, but I really don't want to. Trouble is, if I don't he's bound to get fed up with me and I don't want him to stop being my boyfriend because having him as Anna's boyfriend feels as comfortable as an old pair of slippers, apart from the snogging issue of course, which feels like a pair of uncomfortable high heels.

Of course Bella would be quite happy to snog Olly but that could never happen. Maybe that's why I don't want Anna to snog him either, because if she did, she might start turning into Bella and that is too weird and scary even to think about. How can a split personality have a split personality? I guess if anyone can do it, I can.

'You know it's my birthday next week,' Eve said cheerily. Of course I knew. Eve is going to be 12, another year closer to being a teenager. I don't want Eve, or Anna, to be teenagers. I want us both to stay 12 until we're 18. That way we can avoid a few years of being spotty and embarrassed.

'Of course I know it's your birthday!' I replied, trying to sound cheery. 'It's on Sunday.' I was glad it was a Sunday. I'm at Mum's on Sundays, so I was Anna.

'I'm doing something on the Friday.'

But I'm BELLA *on Friday!!!!!* Luckily I didn't say that out loud. I screamed it in my head. Out loud I just gave a little squeal.

'Are you OK?' asked Eve, concerned.

'Yeah, fine. Just pricked my finger.'

I HAD actually pricked my finger, but I didn't feel as if I'd only pricked my finger. I felt as if I'd been pricked in the heart.

THREE

I know it sounds mad, but the only way I've been able to cope with Mum and Dad splitting up is to never EVER change the days I'm with them: not for Christmas, not for birthdays, not even if I'm in one house and there's vanilla cheesecake in the other.

At first we tried to work it out 'organically', as Mum called it. I called it a mess. We had a vague plan of where I would be each night, but it kept changing, according to Dad's work, Mum's mood and my social life. If Eve was having a sewing sleepover I'd go to Mum's, if Jenny had theatre tickets I'd go to Dad's, but then I'd end up more in one house than the other. We ended up doing complicated calculations of averages and 'nights owed', and I ended up having to stay at Dad's for nine nights on the trot and I missed out on going camping with Mum. Don't get me wrong, I like staying at Dad's, but I also like sitting round the campfire eating sticky marshmallows and melting the toes of my trainers.

So now we have a strict and immutable schedule: Monday, Wednesday and Friday I'm at Dad's; Tuesday, Thursday and Sunday I'm at Mum's. Saturdays alternate between the two but we never alternate the alternating and do two in a row at one house and then two at the other. We tried that once and I got so stressed I came out in spots. Goodness knows, at this crucial pre-teen time I don't need stressy spots on top of the ones that my partly-supressed hormones are kindly giving me.

After Eve had delivered the terrible blow about Friday we kept sewing but I think we both knew this was a difficult moment. The sewing probably helped us avoid eye contact while we sorted it all out.

'Couldn't you change your days?' asked Eve hopefully.

'You know I can't. Could you maybe change your party?'

'No,' said Eve quietly. I can tell she's upset when she goes quiet.

When she whispers she's about to cry, which makes it hard to avoid because you can't hear what she's saying and therefore can't cheer her up.

'I've got tickets for *Streamdance*.'

'Is that the Irish dance show?'

'Yes,' she whispered, 'it's on at the Civic on Friday.'

The Civic's a big old, grey building, probably built around the time grey was a fashionable colour for buildings. It's our local theatre but it's used for lots of other types of show as well. They have films, comedians, beer festivals and folk music from the Ukraine. It's got all the trimmings you find in theatres: a huge red carpet with gold patterns on it, a kiosk selling big packets of fruit pastilles, a bar selling expensive drinks and ladies with big hairdos selling programmes.

I love going there to watch shows, not just because I enjoy the shows, but because it gives me the chance to daydream about BEING in a show there one day. Since I've been to Spotlight, and since I've realised how much I have to act in my everyday life just to maintain my two personalities, I've nurtured a little private dream to be an actress in a REAL spotlight one day. I haven't told anyone yet. I think I'll tell everyone the good news when I get my first TV series.

As far as I know this is the first time they've ever had Irish dance on at the Civic. Eve's mad on Irish dance and a total star at it. She's been going to classes since she was six. She wanted me to come along but I didn't fancy those black tights. Reminded me of old films about boarding school. Eve very bravely went on her own and she's been going to classes ever since. She goes in for competitions and wins prizes which stand proudly on the mantelpiece in her house alongside her mum's bowling trophies. The dancing hasn't just taught her to dance; it's taught her to do amazing things with her hair. She scrunches it into all kinds of buns and pleats, and finishes it off with bows and glitter. She's tried out styles on me, but it's not really worth it because I have to pull them all out when I go back to Dad's. I'm not a 'bows in the hair' kind of person at my Dad's.

'Couldn't you get tickets for another night?' I asked gently.

She sniffed. 'No – the only night it's on is Friday. It's a tour and they do 20 places in 15 days.'

'Wow! How do they find time to wash their tights?' I teased.

'It's not funny. Are you coming or not?' she said, dead serious.

'OK, I'll come,' I said, but as the words left my mouth my stomach turned, as if it wanted to leave my body too. Eve's whole face broke into a smile. She put down her sewing and gave me a hug. Words flooded out of her as if they'd been dammed up by disappointment.

'It'll be brilliant, we've got seats right at the front and Mum says we can go for pizza before and ice-creams during and a sleepover afterwards. I could do your hair! What are you going to wear? I'm going to wear my black dress and black tights.'

Black tights again. I wouldn't be wearing those; I still felt sick and it wasn't because of the tights. Despite how I felt, I tried to look pleased and I think I probably convinced her that I was. I was the only one who knew how bad my life had become: not only would I have to tell Dad the terrible news that I wasn't going to be with him on Friday, I would have to tell my other best friend Jenny, AND I would miss the Spotlight auditions. I realised I wouldn't even be able to enjoy Eve's birthday because of what I was missing. Of course I know you can't be in two places at once, but sometimes you can't even be in one place at once if you're thinking about the other place all the time.

I was quite glad to get back to Dad's on Monday so I could talk to Jenny all about it, except that I couldn't tell Jenny all about it because she doesn't know about Eve. When I met Jenny at secondary school we clicked from day one, well from minute one. I saw her in the playground as we lined up to go in and I really liked her shoes. I know that sounds a superficial reason for deciding someone's going to be your best friend, but it wasn't *just* her shoes. They were an indication of the rest of her – smart, fun and a bit different – and once I got to know her she was in fact just like her shoes, apart from the fact she's not made of leather.

I held back about Eve at first because I was so taken up with making friends with Jenny, and the longer I didn't tell her about Eve, the harder it got. So although she knows

I have friends from primary school I still see, she doesn't know I have another best friend. This made telling her about next Friday totally tricky; I had to say my mum wanted me to go to the opening of a patchwork exhibition.

'Patchwork! Bella, are you out of your not-at-all tiny mind? You can't! You musn't! You shouldn't! You won't!' Jenny was lounging on my dad's huge white L-shaped sofa. She had her long legs flung over the end and was throwing raisins in the air, trying to catch them in her mouth. She didn't catch any, but she kept doing it.

'I should really,' I said limply, not at all like Bella.

'You can't! You musn't! You shouldn't! You won't!' she screeched again, as if saying it again would convince me.

'But . . .' I tried.

'Bella,' said Jenny severely, as she swung her legs to the floor and sat up straight. This meant she was serious, because she loves lounging around more than anything, even buying jeans. 'This is our big chance! We've been planning this for ever . . .'

'Since last week,' I ventured. She bristled at my little reference to her exaggeration and retorted:

'Are you saying you don't want to do the audition?'

'No!' I exclaimed and then told her truthfully, 'I want to be able to be in two places at once.'

'Right,' said Jenny decisively and I could almost see her thinking. She shut her big brown eyes and her long, well-mascaraed lashes rested gently on her cheeks. She tucked her dark brown bob behind her ears and put her hands on her knees. This was concentration, big-time. After a few seconds she snapped her eyes open.

'I've got it!' and she gave me one of her big, winning smiles. 'You can't be in two places at the same time, but you *can* be in one place for half the time, twice.' She looked at me as if I must know what she meant, and I looked at her to show her that I didn't. 'You ask to audition first, you ring your mum and say you've been held up, then you do your audition, rush off to your mum's scratchwork—'

'Patchwork.'

'Whatever. You keep everyone happy.'

Jenny was right, as so often. Her plan would work and I would follow it, except that I wasn't going to the exhibition with Mum, I was going to *Streamdance* with Eve.

After we'd decided on the plan we got down to watching *A Bug's Life* DVD. We'd both seen the film loads of times before but we still love it. I like watching things I used to watch when I was younger because it makes me realise how much older I am now but also reminds me of when I was little. It's one of the few times I feel like a whole person, not a person split in two. I wish I felt like that more often, but there's only so many films like *A Bug's Life* you can watch, even at Christmas.

'I think I should go for the Queen,' said Jenny as we watched, 'because I think I have those same qualities of maturity and wisdom.'

'And modesty,' I teased.

'Which part are you going to audition for?'

'I don't know.'

'Well I do. You should go for Princess Atta.'

'Jenny! Are you out of your not-at-all tiny mind?'

'Totally not.'

'Totally not, what?'

'Not out of my not-at-all-tiny-and-really-quite-impressive mind.'

'But she's the one who falls in love,' I bleated. 'I'll have to kiss a boy with everyone watching.'

'It'll be practice for the end of year disco,' said Jenny knowingly.

FOUR

Friday came and at 6pm my complicated timetable began. I met Jenny on our corner, which is the corner where we always meet. It's exactly half-way between Dad's flat and Jenny's house, we worked it out on a map website. Jenny always gets there before I do; I think it's because she's got bigger feet and so takes bigger strides and walks faster. Or it could be because I always leave late.

As I approached her I could see she was dressed entirely in green. She looked a bit like a lime lollipop. I had to comment.

'Has your mum been dyeing again?'

'She looked fine when I left home,' said Jenny, deadpan.

'I mean *clothes* dyeing,' I said, indicating her green garb.

'No way,' Jenny answered, a bit affronted. 'This was my idea. It's psychology.'

'Are you trying to make everyone else at Spotlight feel ill?'

'No!' she retorted. 'It's a sub-conscious message to Rich. If I wear green it'll plant the seed in his mind that I look like an ant and he'll choose me.'

'Ants aren't green.'

'They are in the film.'

'True. Do you think it'll work?'

'Well I used the same idea to get a date with Marcus from the football team. He supports Newcastle so I wore their colours.'

'And it worked?'

'Kind of. He asked me if I could get hold of any tickets.'

'To take you?'

'To take Jasmine, actually, but it got us talking.'

As we turned the corner into the road the hall is in, we saw Tamara. She's one of the youngest in Spotlight and she's really sweet. She's just right for Dot, Princess Atta's little sister, and she was wearing a ra-ra skirt with dots on (maybe she had the same approach as Jenny and she thought the 'dots' would make Rich think of 'Dot').

The skirt was just like one that Eve bought Anna for Christmas and I was just about to say how cute it was when Jenny said: 'Just look at what she's wearing!' under her breath. 'That skirt is just so totally last year,' Jenny went on, 'I don't know how she can bear to wear it. It's out, out, out. Do you think I should tell her?'

'No,' I said quietly, feeling a chill run through me despite the warm evening. It was a cool reminder that my two best friends were so different. If they did ever meet they wouldn't get on. No wonder I'd kept them apart.

Spotlight is held in St Stephen's church hall, which is totally crumbling and bashed up. Still, I guess many a glamorous actress, who stars at the glitzy Civic, started off in a drama club held in a run-down church hall like St Stephen's.

If there were a prize for the most run-down church hall, St Stephen's would have to win it. The paint's peeling so much you can see every colour the walls have been, almost back to the days of the Bible. The floor is scuffed with the footmarks of all the groups who use the hall: our drama club, the brownies, yoga, under 5s fitness, and over 50s fitness; I don't know what you're supposed to do if you're over 5 and you want to be fit, apart from wait until you're 50.

Despite the depressing venue, we always have a great time. We do warm-up exercises, like walking around with our eyes shut and having to guess who we bump into by feeling their shoes. We do trust games, like jumping off the stage and letting everyone else catch us, which usually works; unless it's Chelsea, who's a show off, we always nearly drop her. We improvise scenes, like a homeless person and the Queen trapped in a lift, or a film star and a girl who works in Boots on a faraway planet.

The highlights are the summer and winter shows. In winter we do something with a Christmas theme, or at least a bit spiritual, even if it's only the story of a nun who became a rock star and then went back to being a nun because she discovered she didn't like loud music. In summer we do big shows that have usually got something to do with Shakespeare, Disney or Cliff Richard.

When we walked in Rich, our director, was sitting astride a chair the wrong way round, so he had his arms leaning on the back of it. He always does that and I once asked him why, and he said he wants to be 'aware'. I can't think what of, except feeling uncomfortable. Rich has floppy hair and falling down jeans. I don't think they're falling down in a fashionable way; I think they're falling down because he's forgotten to put on a belt.

Ralph and Jimmy were sitting at the other end of the hall, so I asked Rich if I could go first. Rich always wants everything to be 'democratic'. He's told us it's because he's the youngest of seven and he never got as much jelly as the others. So, typically, he asked the two who had arrived before us if they minded if I went first. Ralph was practising pulling faces in a pocket mirror. I'm not sure that's the best way to improve your acting skills but he wanted to do a few more, so he was happy to let me go ahead of him. Jimmy's a really rough boy who grunts instead of talking. When Rich asked if he minded if I went first he did one of his grunts and we assumed that meant he didn't mind. Rich said 'cool' at my rendition of the Princess but I didn't really believe it because he says cool all the time because he thinks it's cool. Not when you're 46 it isn't.

Jenny's comment about Anna's skirt (even though she didn't know it was Anna's skirt) had left me feeling a bit shaky and insecure. When Rich told me he wanted me to improvise as well as read from the script I felt even worse.

'So, Princess Atta, how do you feel about being the Queen?' asked Rich. I took a deep breath. That was a deep Bella breath. Then I took a deep Atta breath and started.

'Well I'm not the Queen yet, you know, so I can't really say how I'll feel about being the Queen until I am the Queen, because you can't tell how something will feel until you actually feel it. Does that answer the question? I guess it does – or maybe it doesn't? I don't know. I guess I don't know about anything.'

I stopped there and looked expectantly at Rich. He wrote a few notes on his pad.

'Thanks, Bella,' was all he said.

'Thanks,' I said back. For what? For listening? For not giving me the part? I was pretty sure I hadn't got it. I must have sounded so unsure about everything, but then Atta's like that. So maybe it was OK. I wasn't sure enough to say.

Now I needed to get on with getting to the

Civic. I made straight for the loos, which luckily were near the front door of the hall. Unluckily Jenny followed me there. Perhaps if I'd have said goodbye in the hall she wouldn't have followed me, but I was totally preoccupied with getting changed for the Civic so I rushed immediately to the loo.

'Are you all right, Bella?' she called from the other side of the door. 'Yeah, fine,' I said, as I tried to take off my Bella clothes as quietly as possible.

'Have a good evening.'

'Yeah, thanks, bye,' I said without thinking.

'It's OK, I'll wait until you come out to say goodbye.'

Help! Just what I didn't want. I was now wearing a ra-ra skirt with stripes, a bit like Tamara's. Jenny would hate it. I quickly thought of a excuse as I swapped my big hoop earrings for little teddy bear ones.

'Isn't it your turn to audition?'

'No. Rich's doing the boys first.'

Just my luck. What could I do to get past

her? Under pressure, inspiration struck. I rattled the lock. 'Oh no!' I said, trying to sound natural, 'The lock's stuck! I'll have to climb out of the window,' I said as I looked up to check that there was a window in the loo and that it was big enough for me to get through it.

'I'll get Rich,' she called over, as I changed out of my wedges and into my flat pumps.

'No, no,' I called back, putting a couple of bunches in my hair and stuffing the Bella clothes and shoes in my bag, 'I haven't got time.'

'Are you sure?' she said doubtfully. I put down the loo cover and climbed onto it.

'Yeah, it's quicker this way. Cool, dude,' I muttered as I climbed out of the window, although the last thing I was feeling was cool.

'Chill, sorted,' I heard her say as I jumped out of the window into the alleyway next to the hall. I straightened my striped skirt as I stood up. Then I started running as fast as I could to the bus stop, glancing behind me only once I was at the end of the street to see if Jenny had followed me out. No. I was safe.

'What am I like?' I said to myself as I slowed down, catching my breath as I neared the bus stop. Running away from one of my best friends just because of how I look? As I hot-footed it to the bus stop I wondered how long this double life would go on. Would I go to two colleges, have two jobs, even two husbands? Imagine getting married twice – it'd be fun having two dresses but it wouldn't be much fun climbing out of the church's loo window to get to the registry office on time. Luckily this horrific daydream was interrupted by the bus's arrival.

I'd decided to ring Eve at the last minute rather than tell her I'd be late, because if I'd told her she'd have made all sorts of plans like giving me a lift, which would have blown everything. I phoned her mobile from the bus and breathlessly told her the bus had broken down and I'd had to wait 30 minutes for the next one. I don't know why that would have made me breathless, but I thought it made the situation seem more real. She said we could eat afterwards and she'd leave my ticket at the box office if I wasn't there by the start of the show.

I ran from the bus stop to the Civic. It looked deserted so I knew the show had started. The programme sellers were sitting on the floor in the foyer, chewing pastilles (probably a freebie from the kiosk) and counting their takings.

I ran over to the box office and because I was a bit breathless (for real this time), I did a bit of a mime to indicate that a ticket had been left for me. The mime must have been reasonably good because the box office attendant plonked a ticket in front of me. She didn't say a word, I guess because she was in the middle of downing a huge glass of wine.

I glanced at the gold clock in the foyer as I made my way to the auditorium. I was seven minutes late for the start of the show. An usher opened the heavy door and lilting Irish music sang out at me. The usher shone a torch in the direction of my row. I nodded thanks and crept into my seat. Eve glanced away from the stage for a nanosecond to acknowledge my arrival. I don't think she was annoyed, she just couldn't bear not to watch every moment of the show.

I really enjoyed it, despite the endless black tights. My thoughts wandered occasionally, wondering if I'd got the part of the Princess, but when Sean Best, the star, lifted up three girls and did a hundred steps to the second at the same time I was so impressed I didn't think about anything else at all.

When it was over, Eve turned and beamed at me. 'That's it. I've decided what I'm going to do with the rest of my life.'

'Marry Sean Best?' I teased.

'No – I want to be in a show like *Streamdance.*'

We linked arms as we left the auditorium, chatting about the show and what topping we would have on our pizzas. Eve's mum was waiting for us in the foyer as arranged. Before we had a chance to tell her about the show I saw a horrific sight on the other side of the foyer: JIMMY from Spotlight, from my other life. He didn't actually look horrific, he looked normal – but it was horrific for me that he was in the same place as Eve. He actually looked a bit shocked, which I guess was because I looked so different. I decided to make a break for it and headed straight for the loo. I seem to spend an awful lot of time in loos these days.

Unfortunately Jimmy followed me and got to the loo before I did.

'Bella,' he said.

'SSssshh!' I said, terrified that Eve would hear. Of course he looked totally taken aback.

'Are you OK?'

'Yes,' I said, trying to think of a reason for my weird behaviour. 'Got a bit of a headache.'

'Oh, sorry. You got the part of the Princess,' he said.

'Did you come here to tell me that?' I asked, genuinely confused.

'No. I've come to pick up my sister,' he explained.

'Oh. Well, thanks,' I replied gruffly.

'Ain't you chuffed?' he asked.

'Yeah, yeah,' I said, totally taken aback not only at the news that I'd got the part but also at seeing him there.

'I'm Flick,' he said and then he did something strange: he smiled. I don't know if it was the first time in his life he'd ever smiled, but it was certainly the first time *I'd* seen him smile.

'Fine,' I said, feeling relieved. Flick is the one who ends up with the Princess. At least I don't fancy Jimmy so that should be OK.

Feeling uncomfortable with the embarrassing collision of my two worlds, I turned round abruptly and walked back to Eve. I wondered if Jimmy had noticed that I'd totally changed my image since I saw him at Spotlight earlier that evening, and what he'd think of me shushing him just because he called me Bella, which he thinks is my name. But I didn't have time to dwell on these thorny questions because when I got back to Eve she was peering at me inquisitively.

Then came the terrifying question, 'Who's he?'

FIVE

I panicked. I guess I could have told Eve he was called Jimmy. I could have told her about Spotlight. I could even have told her about the auditions, but that would be the crunch. She'd want to come to the show, and then she'd meet all my other friends, and find out all about the different me, right down to the fact that I chew different gum. With Jenny I have menthol because it's cool; with Eve I have bubblegum because I always have.

I didn't have time to think all this but my instincts went into overdrive. I vaguely and unconvincingly said, 'Don't know.'

I was right about the unconvincing bit because she immediately said, 'Then how come he said, "You've got the part"?'

'I don't know. He must be mad.' I felt a bit bad about saying this because it wasn't true and I don't like to be dishonest, except when it comes to my personalities. I don't really like it even then, but 'needs must', as Mum says when she has a biscuit.

Eve kind of believed me. She kept glancing suspiciously in his direction as we left the theatre, as if he might suddenly do something really mad, like nick a poster for the show from off the wall. He didn't, of course, because he's not mad. He studiously looked the other way and I did the same. This didn't quite work because we somehow crossed over in the crowd coming out of the theatre; as we were both looking the other way we ended up looking straight at each other. My only option then was to do that pathetic thing of pretending I had something in my eye, which I actually did: my finger. I rubbed so hard I looked like Eve after she's watched a weepie. Well, half of me did.

I managed to get back to normal over the pizza, well as normal as I ever get, which is *thinking* about being two people, instead of panicking about being two people. Being genuinely normal, Eve really enjoyed the evening and I think she forgot about the Jimmy incident; the dough balls and the silly waiters helped. One of them even juggled with dough balls, although not mine, I'm glad to say. Eve's mum dropped me back at Dad's and I managed to get into my bedroom without him seeing my Anna clothes.

He was fussing over his tomato plants so he didn't bother to look up. He's been going to a gardening class this year but it hasn't really improved his gardening skills. Everything he planted died, until he tried tomatoes. They're shooting up all over the flat and he tends them obsessively all the time. It's like he's telling them to grow. I've tried to do the same with my boobs: I give them a good talking-to every night but it's not worked so far.

As soon as I got into my Bella bedroom I checked my mobile for texts. I do that about a hundred times a day. I even check first thing in the morning when I've checked last thing at night. I don't know what I'm expecting, except maybe a text from a different time zone, like Australia. But the only person I know from there is Kylie Minogue and I don't think she's got my number.

There was a text! From Jenny, of course. Jenny texts me all the time, even when I'm with her. It means we can chat more, because we talk and text at the same time. Jenny's text was only three words long but they were dead exciting: 'I'm the Queen!' said the text. So she'd got the part she was after. Now we were both going to be royals, even though it was only royal ants.

On Saturday afternoon I went to Mum's via the nutty clothes shop. The dog was still in the window and the shop was still empty.

'Hi there,' called the woman's voice from behind the curtain.

'Hi,' I managed back this time. I didn't even pretend to look at the clothes. I dived behind the screen, managed not to tread on the cat, and pulled my Anna clothes out of my bag. As I tugged them on I caught sight of myself in the mirror. The smart little shirt I'd been wearing at Dad's looked mad with the baggy jeans I'd put on for Mum's. One half of my straw-blond, scarecrow hair was down, and the other was still up in the bunches I'd had at Mum's. I grimaced at the ridiculousness of the situation, at the ridiculousness of me.

When I was ready I went back out into the shop and noticed a new plant by the door. It was like a twirly, twisted hedge and there was a red and yellow plastic flower stuck in the top of it. Had it been there when I arrived and I hadn't noticed it? Or had the owner popped out and put it there when I was behind the screen? I hadn't heard anything, but then I'd been rustling around with my clothes. It was very odd, but no odder than me.

'Bye,' I called as I left, taking the initiative.

'See you soon,' she called back. How did she know I'd be back? In any case, she wouldn't see me if she never actually came out into the shop.

Life went back to normal for a couple of days, well, as normal as my life ever is, until Parents' Evening. Now Parents' Evening is not normally a problem, because Mum doesn't go. This is not because she doesn't care or because I've banned her for wearing a patchwork waistcoat; it's because she thinks there's too much fuss about school. She says school is for the school day and the rest of the day should be ours.

Trouble is, Dad thinks the total opposite. He thinks school is completely important. He's always trying to help with my home-work, and telling me to watch 'educational' programmes when *Hollyoaks* is on. Worst of all, he ran the raffle for the new toilets fundraiser. First prize was one of his pathetic tomato plants. Please!

I went along to Parents' Evening with Dad, feeling fine. It was the second one at my secondary school so we'd got the hang of going to see all the different subject teachers and then my form tutor. The feedback was just what I thought it would be: great for art and drama, OK for French and sport and 'Hello, is there anybody in there?' for everything else.

Then we came to Mr Collins my form tutor. He's a bit like my dad: wears black all the time and has such a small beard you can't work out what he's trying to hide. I certainly didn't have time to work it out there and then because my eyes were drawn to the other side of the room where my fantasy footballer, Remi, had joined the queue to see the PE teacher. With his handsome dad standing behind him, Remi proved himself much more real than any fantasy by turning his curly head towards me and giving me a slow, subtle but unmistakeable smile. I looked quickly around me to see if anyone nearby had fainted with happiness but they were all still standing and conscious.

Then I did something totally uncool. Still in disbelief that the smile was for me, I pointed at myself in a really stupid way, as if to say, 'You mean me?' He smiled AGAIN and nodded and then, cruelly, our rapidly growing relationship was cut off by my father almost shouting, 'Bella!' at me.

'That's me,' I replied dreamily.

'So have you any ideas?'

'About what?' I answered dreamily.

'About why your homework is so inconsistent,' said Mr Collins as he held up a few books. 'This was excellent, this was poor, this was brilliant, this was patchy.' He pointed at the work as he spoke. 'There seems to be no pattern, sometimes work in the same subject differs wildly in standard.'

Dad looked at me; I looked at Dad. We

both knew exactly why. I wasn't going to let on, but I knew Dad *wanted* the teacher to find out.

'Have you noticed any difference according to *when* the homework's done?' he asked Mr Collins, trying to sound all innocent.

'You mean she may have had a bad week?' asked Mr Collins.

'A bad *day*,' said Dad pointedly. 'Or a few bad days. The same days every week.'

It didn't take long for the penny to drop. My good homework is done on the days I'm at Dad's; the bad homework on the days I'm at Mum's.

'Ah,' said Mr Collins, 'so perhaps we need to have a word with Mum.' Dad looked triumphant.

'There's no point,' I said quickly. 'Mum doesn't believe in homework.'

'That doesn't make any difference. Unlike God, there is proof of homework's existence whether we believe in it or not,' said Mr Collins, brandishing an exercise book. He teaches Religious Studies so he's good on God.

'OK, I'll sort it out,' I said vaguely, not wanting Dad to get involved. Also, I'd just seen Jenny go by and I was desperate for a chat. Her parents were trailing behind her, having a laugh. Jenny says they're boring because they always agree about everything, but I'd love my parents to be a bit more boring.

Mum doesn't actually try to stop me doing my homework, but she certainly doesn't believe in *helping* your children with their homework. Dad makes up for that lack of faith many times over.

I don't know if he does it to compensate for Mum, but ever since I can remember I've had posters by my bed about numbers, letters, planets and monarchs. I've even got a poster about posters.

Dad isn't even reluctant about helping me. He dives on my school bag as soon as I get in the door and looks for my homework book. Then he's off: looking on the internet, planning revision, collecting milk bottle tops. These efforts look even more extreme compared to Mum's minus effort.

It's not that she doesn't want to help me. If it's something that interests her she's amazing. Like when we had to draw a picture of a plant for art, I had a glance round the kitchen and plumped for the spider plant on the fridge. But Mum wouldn't let me start until she'd brought every house plant into the kitchen so I could have a better choice. By the time she'd finished I felt as if I were lost in a tropical jungle with a mad woman chanting at me, but it was only Mum reciting all the latin names.

I got a 5 for that piece of work but when I do well Mum doesn't think the marks I get are for her like Dad does: he was so proud he got a 5 for French he went out and bought some croissants.

At Spotlight on Friday we had our first readthrough of the *A Bug's Life* stage version. I was still replaying the Remi encounter at Parents' Evening in my mind when I had ANOTHER embarrassing boy moment.

We were all sat in a circle reading the lines out loud. Until now I'd only seen the film umpteen times and read the audition pieces. Rich handed out the script and as soon as I got mine I had a flick through it, mainly to see how much I had to say. When I got to the last page I saw a horrendous stage direction: FLICK AND PRINCESS ATTA KISS. Help. It's bad enough getting used to kissing boys, but to have to do it in front of all my drama group and an audience of parents was totally scary.

I looked over at Jimmy who was sitting on the other side of the circle. He was doing exactly the same as me: looking at the last page. So he was finding out the horrible truth too. Then he did something bizarre. He looked up from the script and smiled at me. What did that mean? Did it mean he actually didn't mind kissing me? Was he relishing the humiliation of watching me squirm? I didn't know and I didn't want to find out.

I'd like to say my life went back to normal after that but when you've got two lives normal isn't something you get very often, if at all. The next crisis was a big one, even though it didn't involve kissing. I was at Dad's on Monday evening: nothing odd about that, I'm always at Dad's on a Monday.

I was doing my homework at the computer on the big white table. It's in front of a huge window and we're on the fifth floor so there's a great view over the park, the river, and every type of building you can think of, even monasteries and public loos.

When I'm working at that table I take regular breaks to daydream. I imagine myself like I am now, only better. What I really mean is older. At Dad's I already feel older than I do at Mum's but when I day-dream I've moved on: I've got bigger boobs, shorter skirts, higher heels. I'm striding into an audition for a major film, all confident but not cocky. As soon as I finish reading the director offers me the part. Heaven. Watch out Keira Knightley here I come.

I was having one of these major day-dreams when Dad muttered, 'Just going out,' ever so casually, as if he were just going to put the rubbish out.

Now Dad is so 'always there' he even tells me when he's going to put the rubbish out. He never leaves me for any longer than that, even though I'm actually 12, and friends like Jenny are left practically all night. OK, so she's got three sisters and one of them's 18, but even so, Jenny's big sister is completely irresponsible because she once let a candle burn through a coffee table. She's at art school so she said it looked 'artistic'. I think it looked 'on fire'.

'Going to put the rubbish out?' I mumbled without looking up, expecting that's what he was doing.

'Er – no,' he said vaguely, 'I'll be a bit longer, back about ten.' Three whole hours!

Where on earth would he go for that long? A cold, scary thought popped into my mind and I had to deal with it before it froze me up.

'Somewhere nice?' I asked, like hairdressers do when they're trying to distract you from the fact they're ruining your hair.

'I hope so,' he said cryptically. The ice was spreading: down my back, into my toes. I had a strong and scary suspicion, did he mean *someone* nice' rather than *somewhere* nice'. This could be the beginning of my worst nightmare: one or both of my parents getting a new partner. I can just about cope with the idea of them splitting up but I can't stand the idea of them being with someone new. I had to see this through, to find out.

'So' – and then my nerve snapped, or maybe I didn't really want to know, not yet – 'have a nice time,' I said.

'Yeah,' he said vaguely, because he was peering at his tomato plants again. Then he picked one plant up and wandered towards the door saying, 'See ya.' Then he left.

I relaxed a bit then. It obviously wasn't a date. You don't take tomato plants on dates. I carried on with my homework which was art. I had to draw the view from my window, in the style of the French painter Monet. I lost myself in the misty patterns I was making, so when my mobile rang it made me jump. I answered it and said, 'Bonsoir,' as if I really was Monet.

'Bonsoir to you too,' said Mum.

'You know you're not supposed to ring me here,' I said, sounding more like a parent than a daughter. I've had to stop both Mum and Dad ringing me when I'm not with them because it causes trouble, even though I've got a mobile.

'I know, but I have to tell you something.'

'Go on then,' I said.

'I won't be here tomorrow when you get home.'

'Couldn't you leave me a note?' I said wearily.

'No, because you might not read it and I want you to know where I'm going.'

'Where are you going?' I asked, because I knew she wanted me to.

'To look at a workshop. The council are setting up a craft centre, and I've applied for a workshop, for my patchwork!'

'Great!' I said lamely.

'Well it will be great because I won't have to sew in your room any more.'

Actually, that did sound great. I started to look forward to having the room to myself, instead of sharing it with mountains of material. We got chatting about giving the room a facelift (even though it hasn't got a face) once it was all mine. Then we chatted generally for a bit, and I confessed I'd missed *EastEnders* which made her go all funny. She always worries about what I'm doing at Dad's. I carried on drawing with one hand while she moaned on a bit and then, without thinking at all properly I muttered, 'Don't worry – he'll be back at ten.'

There was a long silence. The full horror

of what I'd said had ample time to sink in. I didn't bother to say anything else because I knew there wasn't any point. Mum never ever leaves me on my own in the evenings. I don't know what she thinks is going to happen. I suppose a gang of thieves could break the door down and threaten to beat us up if we don't hand over our junk jewellery, but I don't think Mum would be much more use in that situation than me.

I went back to my drawing once Mum hung up. It was dark now and I put in a few winking streetlights. It's not that easy to draw something winking but I had a go. I was so involved in what I was doing I didn't hear a car draw up to the flats. I didn't see anyone get out. I didn't think who was knocking at the door before I opened it. I wish I had: it was Mum.

SIX

I didn't even think about what I was wearing, but it was more what I wasn't wearing that was the problem. There was nothing much between my chest and my navel because I was wearing a very cut-off t-shirt and a very low-slung pair of jeans. Mum stared at my stomach. *'At least she's not looking at my shoes,'* I thought, and then she looked at my shoes.

When I'm staying in at Dad's I sometimes wear clothes even I wouldn't dare wear in the street. I've got a couple of pairs of really high-heeled shoes that I took over to Dad's from my old dressing up box at Mum's.

Mum used to wear high heels, before she gave up men.

Mum stopped staring down at the shoes and looked back up at my chest. I made a pathetic attempt to pull down my t-shirt.

'Aren't you cold?' asked Mum with a frown.

'I will be if I stand here any longer,' I said, frowning back.

'Those shoes aren't good for your feet,' she said, not moving.

'I only wear them sitting down,' I said.

'You're standing up,' she said back.

Then Dad came back. He was still clutching the tomato plant and I'm sure it had grown since he took it out.

'Hi,' he said to Mum, 'your hair's longer.'

If I'd had 20 questions to guess what he might say I'd never have guessed that. I'd have guessed, *What the hell are you doing here*? or *I've only been out for a couple of hours and anyway, it's none of your business what I do when Bella's here!* Something like that, but no, it was a little comment about her hair.

'Yes,' she answered, which seemed an obvious thing to say but adults do that, don't they, like telling you you've grown all the time. I thought maybe the conversation was over and I began to feel a surge of relief: there'd been no shouting like there'd been for weeks on end when they were splitting up. I'm not exaggerating, they once had a row about the central heating for ten days.

More fool me for thinking it was over, it had only just begun. Mum pursed her lips together but let a few words out, 'So you're back.'

'So it would seem,' replied Dad, equally terse.

'And do you have any kind of plan?' asked Mum.

'What for? Retirement? A holiday?' Dad was being difficult but Mum wasn't exactly being easy.

'For what our daughter would do if anything happens to you while you're out.'

'I'm always on the mobile.'

'What if there's no signal?'

'She can always ring you.'

'What if I'm out?'

'What about *your* mobile?'

'What if there's no signal?' They went on like that for a while, getting crosser and crosser until Mum shouted what she really thought.

'I THINK IT'S TOTALLY IRRESPON-SIBLE TO LEAVE A 12-YEAR-OLD HOME ALONE!'

And Dad shouted back, 'AND I THINK IT'S NONE OF YOUR BUSINESS WHAT I DO WHEN SHE'S WITH ME!'

All in all I wish they'd gone on talking about Mum's hair.

Next day, I didn't tell Jenny about my parents' row. Her parents get on with each other really well; in fact they get on so well they actually GO OUT together. Admittedly they only go out to classes that tell them how to get on with each other, but it's better than nothing, and it's certainly better than my parents, who only went out together to classes on how to split up.

When I arrived in the playground Jenny was already standing around watching the football. She doesn't actually look like she's watching the football: that would be uncool. She looks like she's looking at her nails, but there's only so long you can do that. In between fiddling with her cuticles she glances up at the football – well, the players. I joined in both activities.

'Hi, dude,' I said casually to Jenny as I took up my position next to her.

'Dude, yourself,' she said back. That's how we always say hello.

'What's the score?' I asked, nodding at the game.

'No idea, but Marcus's underpants get my top marks.' Marcus even plays football with his trousers slung frighteningly low, and despite this hindrance he still manages to kick the ball.

I didn't look at him for long. It was too worrying because it really looked like his trousers were going to fall round his ankles. Instead, I got on with ogling Remi. It was hard not to stare, and I don't just mean at his 100 per cent dreamy good looks. It was actually hard not to gawp open-mouthed at the way he plays football. I don't actually like football, when Dad watches it I never ever sit watching it with him, even though he'd probably love it if I did. I'm not trying to be mean; I just hate the way football drowns out everything else when it's on. The *Match of the Day* theme tune makes me feel slightly sick.

Watching Remi is something else. He runs with the ball at his feet, twisting and turning, but keeping the ball with him. It's as if there's an invisible elastic between him and the ball and even if the ball strays a few inches from his feet it soon comes back to where it belongs.

I think I must have been staring at Remi without realising because all of a sudden the ball was kicked off the pitch and he came running towards it – and me. I quickly stopped staring at him and went back to staring at my nails. The ball hit the fence just next to Jenny and me.

Remi grabbed it and as he turned to throw it back on he said the most magic word to me: 'Hi.'

I would have been happy to stand there and relish the moment for a few hours more but Jenny spoilt it by giving me a huge dig in the ribs. I spent the rest of the day wondering if he'd noticed and if it mattered if he had and what it all meant anyway.

Why was I being so *teenage* about Remi? I'm not even 13 until June. Once I'm 13 I can expect to go all hopeless and speechless (but never braless if I'm Bella because of the tissues) but while I'm still 12 I should be a bit more mature. It didn't take long for me to answer my own interrogation. I couldn't pretend to myself that I was interested in Remi because of his left foot. You can't snog a left foot. You can't hold hands with it. You can't put your arms round it. Remi was filling up my mind but not leaving it so full that I could completely forget about Olly.

Although it was Bella who was falling for Remi and Anna who was going out with Olly, it still didn't feel right. Why was I letting Bella's feelings for Remi escalate, when Anna already had an almost *too* steady boyfriend? Or maybe it was all OK because two people can have two boyfriends and there's two of me so I can have two boy-friends too. I stopped troubling myself about these thorny dilemmas when I reminded myself that Bella wasn't actually going out with Remi so I didn't need to worry – not yet anyway.

So Bella stopped worrying about Remi, but then Anna started worrying about Olly. The next Saturday I was just getting my stuff out for the weekly sewing binge with Eve when Olly did his morse code ring at the door.

'You're early,' I said, because he always seems to come round when Eve is there.

'Fancy a walk?' he asked.

'To the park?' I asked back, knowing that 'park' was a code word for 'snog'.

'If you want to,' he said. I didn't want to, really. Snogging someone new like Remi was one thing, but snogging my little school boyfriend . . . it didn't feel comfy and safe like Anna likes to feel.

'Eve's coming round soon, I haven't got time.' This was true, but it was a good excuse as well.

'A quick walk, then?'

'OK.'

We set off round the block. He held my hand.

'How's the painting going?' I asked.

'Tricky. I'm doing beards and I don't know how many soldiers had them.'

'Loads, I bet. It can't be easy to shave in the middle of a battle.'

'True. Maybe they should all have beards.'

'Apart from the generals. They probably had time to shave.'

'Trouble is, beards are tricky to paint.'

'Does it really matter?' I was a bit irritated with this conversation. There's a limit to how interested I can be in painting Napoleonic soldiers. Still, it was a good deterrent from talking about what I knew Olly wanted to talk about. He still managed it, though.

'So – do you *ever* want to go to the park?'

'Er . . . yeah. Great,' I said miserably. I suppose Anna had to grow up a bit sometime. When you're 12 you can't go out with someone and never snog. It's all right when you're 11 but not once you've hit secondary school. If I didn't snog Olly soon I wouldn't be able to call him my boyfriend any more.

'When shall we go, then?' he persisted.

'Soon.'

'OK.'

We arrived back at my front door just as the conversation ended. He let go of my hand.

'See ya then,' he said and wandered off.

'See ya,' I said back. I watched him go and wondered why he hadn't even given me a peck on the cheek. He's so good at those. Maybe he was withholding kissing services until we did it properly. I shuddered at the thought. Then I shuddered again. What on earth was *really* wrong with me? Did Anna have that much of a problem with snogging? Or did Anna have a problem with snogging Olly?

Bella certainly didn't share Anna's concerns in the snogging department. She could hardly stop herself from daydreaming about kissing Remi. In fact, during break on the next Monday at school I was standing on the sideline having a nice long daydream about Remi when Remi himself trotted over to pick up a stray ball and interrupted it.

'Hi there,' he said as he bent down to grab the ball. I looked around to see who he might be talking to, but there wasn't anyone else around. Jenny had gone to the loo and most of the other girls were plaiting their hair.

'Hi,' I said back. I had a good look at

him as he stood up. He has the dreamiest chocolate-coloured eyes and gorgeous, smooth skin.

'Fancy coming to the next match?' he asked.

'Yeah,' I said before I had time to think if I did or not. Luckily when I thought about it afterwards I decided I'd given the right answer.

'I'll meet you here, two on Saturday.' Then he was off, back to the game. I don't think any of the other boys even noticed he'd said anything to me.

Was this a date? I know it wasn't the cinema, or chips, or a walk in the park, but he'd still asked me OUT somewhere. OK, it was to football, but that meant he'd be showing me off to all his friends, unless of course he didn't like what I was wearing and then he could pretend I was a saddo who'd turned up and had nothing to do with him. I texted Jenny with my exciting news while she was still on the loo.

*

I had the rest of the week to plan what I was going to wear and I needed it, not to decide on the outfit but to work out how I was going to get it on. I was at Dad's on Friday so I left there on Saturday morning with Anna clothes in my bag. I stopped at the nutty clothes shop, changed, went to Mum's, then after lunch I went *back* to the clothes shop to change *back* into Bella clothes to go and meet Remi.

When I went to the nutty clothes shop the second time the owner was actually there! I didn't realise until I got into the shop. I was so used to the shop being empty I'd marched in and was practically behind the screen before I realised that I was not alone.

A tall woman with long red hair was standing by a little round table. She was wearing a long black coatdress and she was arranging daffodils in a big antique jug.

'Sorry,' I blurted as soon as I saw her.

'Why? Have you pinched something?' she said, without looking round.

'No!' I said defensively. 'But I was going

to use the changing room without buying anything.'

'Feel free,' said the nutty shop lady. 'I do it all the time.'

So with her permission I scooted behind the screen and got changed. When I came out looking completely different she didn't even turn round for a look. I began to feel miffed that she wasn't more interested in me and then I realised that her lack of interest was a good sign because it meant I could go on changing there.

When I got to school Remi was standing waiting for me at the gates. That felt like a proper date, even though we were only going to a school football match. He looked fantastic, in wine- and gold-coloured kit that toned beautifully with his hair.

'Hi,' he said, 'you look good.'

'Hi,' I said back, 'so do you.'

Hallelujah! I'd spent ages deciding what to wear, because I wanted to look special, but I also wanted to look like I'd made no effort at all. So the torn jeans and off the shoulder t-shirt had done their work, along with the tough but feminine boots I was wearing.

We walked over to the pitch. I wanted to hold hands but felt it was too early in the relationship for that kind of intimacy. As soon as Remi's toe touched the sideline he was into football mode. He trotted over to his friends, did a whole load of high fives and then launched into a punishing sequence of warm-up exercises.

I stayed on the sidelines, ready to cheer. There weren't many other people there, just a few keen parents and a couple of other girlfriends – not that I was a girlfriend – yet.

The other team were a shabby lot. Their kit was either too big or too small and they trotted around, looking exhausted before they'd even started, unlike our frisky team. Remi raced all over the pitch, whether he had the ball or not, and it wasn't long until he tackled one boy, dodged another, pushed another out of the way and booted the ball straight into the back of the net.

I cheered loudly. I even jumped up and

down a bit. So did the other girls, so I knew it was the right thing to do. Remi did a cartwheel. The other players came over and ruffled his hair. Then he came over and flung his arms around me. That felt fantastic, even though he was quite sweaty. A couple of the parents took photos. It was looking good. Remi was looking good. The future for Remi and me was looking good.

We won 6–1. Remi scored a hat trick and got the Man of the Match Award. I cheered as loudly as anyone. At the end of the match he trotted towards me. I was wondering what would happen now, would he walk me home, or would we go for a drink, or something to eat?

'Sorry,' he said. 'Got to have a team talk.'

'Oh,' I said.

'But thanks for coming. You looked really good.'

'Thanks,' I said, flattered.

'It was good to see you out of uniform.'

'You too!' I replied, as cheerily as I could.

Inside I was disappointed that the date

was ending there and then. Remi trotted back to the team and I left. On the way home I texted Jenny with every detail of the 'date'. It cost a fortune but it was worth it. In fact it was almost better telling Jenny than actually being at the match.

Four whole days went by and Remi hadn't asked me on the next date. Mind you, I hadn't asked him either. Perhaps he was waiting for me to make that move. I tried to dream up a few suitable dates, but I couldn't decide between shopping for clothes and shopping for shoes.

But on Thursday evening I got into major boy trouble. I was round at Mum's so I was being Anna and I was drawing. Bella likes to draw too but if she's got the choice she draws boys and Anna draws kittens. I was lost in my drawing when the doorbell rang. I wasn't expecting anyone and Mum was in the bath so I looked out of the window. It was Eve! She never normally comes round in the week so I was worried there was a problem. I hurried to the door to open it.

There clearly was a problem. She looked cross and upset and disappointed all at once. She was holding up the local newspaper. It was open at the sports pages and there was a big photo of Remi with his arms around me at the football match. Underneath the headline read: JUNIOR JUBILATION!

I tried desperately to think of something to say but she beat me to it.

'Who,' she said sternly, 'is THIS?'

SEVEN

It was bad luck, really. One of the parents had sent a photo to the local paper. Eve was looking for boot sale information. She flicked through the local paper and saw the photo.

Eve got all huffy about it, as if I'd been two-timing *her* not Olly. I'm sure Bella would have been able to cleverly talk her out of her huff, but Anna got all flustered.

'I was going to tell him,' I fibbed.

'Well now you don't have to because I already have,' she said, all tight-lipped.

'That wasn't very loyal of you,' I retorted.

'Well it wasn't very loyal of you to go off with someone else,' said Eve, all superior and trying to sound like a teen mag agony aunt.

'I haven't "gone off" with him. I watched him play football!' I squealed.

'Yeah, but you were going to go off with him, weren't you?'

'Not necessarily.'

Eve sniffed, even though she hadn't got a cold. I suddenly felt really irritated with her. She was acting all superior and like she knows all about relationships, and frankly, the nearest she's got to a relationship is a cuddle with her rabbit.

'You know what I mean,' she muttered. Of course I did know what she meant, so I got all defensive.

'I would have told Olly if it had gone any further.'

'What, you mean, just before he reads about your wedding in the local paper?'

'What are you talking about? Remi only asked me to watch him play football!'

'You know what I mean,' she muttered again. I felt like I should at least ask her in but I didn't really want to. We carried on talking on the doorstep.

'I'll go and see Olly, sort things out,' I offered, to patch things up. Then she took a deep breath and said:

'I don't want to get at you, but things have gone all funny. All – secretive. That strange boy at the theatre, and now *this* boy, and I feel – you don't tell me everything any more.'

She was right, of course, and this was just the tip of the iceberg. I didn't know what to say, so I just returned the question, 'Well, do you tell me everything?'

'Yes,' she said, looking up at me so I could see her sweet, open face. I knew that would be the answer. It made me feel worse.

I had to do something about all this: it was all right me being weird, but I didn't want everyone else to feel weird too.

When Eve had gone I went round to Olly's. He only lives a few streets away, in a run-down house that needs painting but has nice coloured glass at the tops of the windows. Olly's dad never gets round to painting the house because he's too busy painting soldiers, like Olly. I guess his mum doesn't do it because she's busy doing all the things the dad would do if he didn't paint soldiers.

I could see Olly as I approached the house because he was painting soldiers in the lounge window. I know he sits there because it's got the best light, and in the winter when it's dark he has a light that pretends it's daylight. It's all very technical. He has the thinnest, daintiest brushes and he dips them in a carefully mixed colour and then makes a tiny spot on the soldier's helmet.

He saw me coming, I know he did, because he half-looked up and then he sort of pretended he hadn't seen me and carried on painting. I wasn't having it. I rang forcefully on the doorbell. He didn't dare ignore that. He leapt up and came to open the door.

'Hi,' he said, as he raised his hand a bit in a half-hearted wave.

'Hi,' I said, 'can I come in?'

'Yeah,' he said, 'but I'll have to keep painting. I can't let this colour dry.' I knew this wasn't an excuse, because I've known Olly long enough to know that paint is expensive and once it's mixed you've got to use it. Nevertheless, it was a good excuse not to look me in the eye.

'I still want to go out with you if you still want to go out with me,' I said, straight out. There's no point beating around the bush with Olly because once the paint's dry he could be off to buy more soldiers.

'We don't go out. Not properly,' he said unhelpfully. I knew he was referring to going up to the park. I felt all defensive again. I tried to argue my way around the problem.

'But we've been calling each other boyfriend and girlfriend for over a year now, and I have said I definitely will go up the park with you.'

'So what are you going to do about *him*? Do you want to go out with him as well?'

'No,' I lied.

'Why not?' asked Olly, bizarrely, as if he were actually encouraging me to go out with Remi. I really, really wanted to tell him that Anna didn't want to go out with Remi at all, that it was Bella who'd gone to the football match, but I knew I couldn't. Instead, I pretended that Anna wasn't too sure about Remi, which was sort of true.

'Well, he's really busy with himself, like he thinks he's the best player in the team and he's got the pick of the girls, and more curls in his hair than I've got freckles on my nose.'

Olly peered at my nose for a moment and then said, rather meanly, 'That's a lot of curls.' That got me going. I was determined to convince Olly that Anna wasn't interested in Remi, so that Bella could then get on with going out with him.

'Why would I want to go out with a big curly-head like him?'

'I know that if you want to go out with him you will, whatever I do or say.'

That got me. I was really upset that I hadn't managed to put him off the scent. He was like my mum when she comes into my room and sniffs the air for traces of hair removal cream. She doesn't approve. She thinks I'm too young to depilate. Well all I can say is that she's too old not to. We're talking upper lip and chin.

I felt like a rat in a trap and that caused me to panic. Instead of backtracking and telling the truth, I dug myself in deeper with a wopping great fib.

'If you really want to know I'm going shopping with him on Saturday and that's when I'm going to tell him I don't want to go out with him!'

'Really?' said Olly, his face brightening a bit.

'Yes, really,' I said back, far too easily. It was as if there was a devil inside me saying all these things, a lying little tapeworm that I couldn't get rid of. I carried on down this dangerous track. 'If you don't believe me you can watch. Four o'clock. Behind the fountain.'

With that I left, leaving the situation far

worse than when I had arrived. What had I done? Well, I'd left behind me a trail of lies and still more that would now have to be told. I hadn't got a date with Remi and if we ever *did* go out no way would I chuck him, but I knew that Olly was so upset that he wouldn't be able to resist a shopping centre showdown.

Now I had a challenge that was beyond even my organisational skills. How on earth was I going to pretend to split up with Remi without actually splitting up with him? It wasn't as if we were really going out, so how could we split up? If I managed to get Remi to go out with me and then tell him we needed to pretend to split up to convince Olly I wasn't going out with him, then Remi would split up with me anyway and that wasn't what I wanted either.

I couldn't crack this one, and I couldn't ask anyone to help me crack it either. Eve would disapprove; Jenny didn't even know about Olly; Mum and Dad didn't know about Remi, and I didn't know what to do.

After four whole days I still hadn't cracked it. I'd written in my diary, I'd read advice columns in teen mags, I'd even eaten some pumpkin seeds because Mum says they're 'brain food'.

It was at Spotlight that inspiration came to me and it was the most unlikely person that inspired me: Jimmy. We were rehearsing our first *A Bug's Life* scene and I have to admit Jimmy's acting was really good.

I had the idea while I was acting with Jimmy but I didn't do anything about it until after the class. I made an excuse to Jenny that I had to buy some lettuce for my dad and scooted off after Jimmy. He was plodding down a side-street, with his collar up and his head down.

'Hi,' I said cheerily, as if it were completely normal for me to follow him down the street.

'Hi, trouble,' he said and almost smiled. He actually has a really nice smile, because he doesn't just smile with his mouth, he smiles with his eyes. They sort of flicker in an amused kind of way, and it makes you notice that his eyes are a rich brown colour and he's got very dark lashes which match his almost black hair. I noticed all this in a nanosecond, and quickly responded.

'I'm not trouble,' I said, then remembered that I was about to be just that, and added, 'Well, not after tonight.'

'Go on then, spill,' he said as he stopped walking. He didn't actually look at me because he kept glancing nervously up and down the street, as if he were embarrassed to be seen with me.

'I need you to do some acting for me. I'll pay you if you like.'

'OK,' he said, without even asking what it was, 'but you don't have to pay me.' To my amazement, he started walking off.

'Don't you want to know what it is?' I exclaimed.

'Yeah, OK,' he said, looking all nervous again. I explained everything, well, not everything because he didn't need to know I have a split personality and I was trying to have two boyfriends. Neither did he need to know that from a distance he could be passed off as Remi. After all, Olly had only seen a fuzzy newspaper photo of Remi and he was so busy hugging me you couldn't really see his face. So I just told Jimmy that I needed him to pretend to be keen on me and then let me chuck him in the Shopping Centre, at four on Saturday.

'OK. I'll see you 3.30, at the fountain,' he said, and then ran off down the street. Strange. He hadn't asked any questions. He didn't seem to think that what I was asking him to do was extremely odd. *I* certainly thought it was extremely odd. I turned and walked back towards the main road. A black limo slid past me and turned smoothly at the end. I wished I could get in it like a film star and slip off to a place where life wasn't so complicated.

EIGHT

I don't really need to describe the Shopping Centre because it's like every other shopping centre: lots of chain stores, security guards, people sitting on benches eating sandwiches. Occasionally there's a flamenco dance demonstration, or a brand new car on display.

In the middle there's a large silver cone, with water running down it. I suppose it's a fountain. People throw coins into the pool at the bottom; I don't know if it's for luck or to get rid of their change.

The Shopping Centre always makes me feel better. I think that's partly because it's where I get anything new in my life, like clothes and lunchboxes, but also because nothing really bad happens there. It doesn't rain, litter is swept up, fights are stopped and old ladies get to sit down.

This time, though, the Centre didn't manage to magically put me in a good mood. It was raining outside and I just felt miserable. I had a hunch that this was because deep down I knew what I was doing was totally stupid.

I was wearing Anna clothes because Olly knew Anna and even though Jimmy knew Bella he'd already seen me as Anna at *Streamdance* and he hadn't said anything about it, so he probably hadn't noticed. Even if he had it didn't matter because he wasn't an important person in my life, so he was never going to find out the truth about me.

Jimmy was sitting by the fountain when I got there. He was still wearing grotty clothes but he looked a bit nicer than usual. Perhaps he'd had a bath, or combed his hair, or something. I didn't dwell on it because

I was thinking about what we had to do.

'Nice t-shirt,' he said. So he did notice my clothes. So why hadn't he said anything at *Streamdance*? Weird. I decided to distract him from me and my image.

'Right. We'd better practise,' I said. 'Let's walk along holding hands.'

'Isn't this a bit weird?' he said. So he did think it was weird. He was right about that.

'Kind of,' I said.

He stood up and took hold of my hand. 'I mean, why do you want to do this?'

'I don't *want* to hold hands.'

'I know. I mean "pretend" like this.'

I started walking along, still holding hands. 'Do I have to say?'

'No,' he answered.

We walked along a bit, looking in the shop windows. It actually felt quite nice. I had a little daydream about kissing him – only in *A Bug's Life* of course. We hadn't rehearsed that bit yet, and it still felt scary. I told myself we'd only be pretending to kiss, like we were pretending to hold hands now, though we actually were holding hands. It was weird to be doing so much pretending with the same boy.

'Is this it?' he said after a bit.

'I suppose you could put your arm round me,' I said vaguely. He immediately did. It felt OK and I wondered if I should put my arm round him. I decided I might as well. I'd just got it in place when a voice behind us said:

'Weird t-shirt.' I knew that voice. It was Remi's. I also knew that the plan had already gone completely and utterly wrong. I immediately dropped my arm from Jimmy's side and turned round. Remi had his arms crossed. He didn't look happy. But why wasn't he at football? I had thought it was safe to do all this stuff because Remi always played football on Saturday afternoon and so wouldn't be in the Centre. But here he was! Standing and glowering at us.

'What are you up to?' he asked.

'Why aren't you at football?' I snapped, like a cross mum.

'It's raining.'

'Don't you play in the rain?' I snapped again.

'The pitch is waterlogged.'

During this bizarre little exchange Jimmy kept his arm round me, and of course I knew why: he thought this was the person he was supposed to be convincing that he was keen on me. Remi suddenly turned round and walked back in the direction he'd come from. I let all the breath I'd been holding in back out. I felt crushed, defeated, and stupid. Remi must think Bella was going out with Jimmy. He would think I'd been two-timing him and he'd clearly gone off me there and then.

Of course Jimmy didn't get it. 'Was that him?' he asked, all innocent.

'No.' I said.

'So we've still got to pretend to have the row?'

'Yes,' I said, thinking about Olly. Bella may have lost Remi but it was still worth convincing Olly that Anna really wasn't going out with anyone else. I started planning: 'I'm going to push your arm away and start rowing.'

'What about?'

'I don't know yet.' I looked at Jimmy and tried to think of something. Maybe I could criticise his hair, or his teeth? Actually, neither of them were that bad, and then I remembered I was supposed to be acting, so I could make something up.

'Well let me know when you're going to start. Give me a little wave or something,' said Jimmy. I tried to think of something to row about, but all I could think was how stupid this whole plan was. It was all designed to let Bella go out with Remi and keep up Anna's relationship with Olly, and now Remi thought Bella was going out with Jimmy! I leant against Jimmy's shoulder and felt a bit despondent.

'What does this bloke look like?' whispered Jimmy.

'Small and dark, like someone who paints soldiers.'

'Is that the geezer?' asked Jimmy, nodding in the direction of the fountain. I looked up and saw Olly, staring madly at Jimmy and me. We were still entwined. We must have been looking totally like a couple. Olly looked very serious. He took something out of his pocket, probably a coin. It could just as well have been a wedding ring. He chucked it in the fountain.

Suddenly it was as if I'd woken up, as if I'd been asleep for the last half hour. I broke away from Jimmy and moved towards Olly. I wanted to explain. It might not be the truth, but it might get him back on my side. As I moved, Olly moved too. Fast. Away. Out of the Centre. That boy may spend most of his life sitting down but he can still move when he wants to.

Why had he gone so quickly? Why hadn't he waited to see me have my row with Jimmy?

'Is that it, then?' said a voice behind me; it was Jimmy.

'Looks like it,' I said, walking back to him.

'So I can go?' he asked abruptly.

'Yup,' I said blankly.

'See ya,' he said.

Then he walked away. I felt really blank and empty. Minutes ago, he'd had his arm round me and we'd been in the middle of a dramatic love triangle and now I was all alone, minus Anna's first ever boyfriend and Bella's exciting new boyfriend. I'd managed to ruin both relationships in one day, quite an achievement. All I could do now was stare at the water slithering down the fountain. I wished I could float away with it.

I decided to share my misery with Jenny so I sent her a long text. I didn't tell her about Jimmy and Olly, I just said that things with Remi had gone very wrong. Then she rang me.

'Hi,' said Jenny brightly, 'I've decided you need cheering up. Where are you?'

'I'm in the Centre, by the fountain,' I answered. 'Where are you?'

'I'm in the Centre too! Up the other end.'

Even though I was pleased to hear her voice I felt all tense. She was in the Centre too! She could have walked by while I was failing to sort out my boy trouble. I'm glad she hadn't seen me cavorting around with Jimmy in my Anna gear.

'Can you come up here?' she asked. I had an ultra-quick think about clothes, luckily I had a Bella outfit in my bag.

'OK,' I said.

'I'll be by leaflet heaven.'

'Cool, dude.'

'Chill, sorted.'

Leaflet heaven is just our name for it. It's really a little kiosk with loads of leaflets on display. They're for all kinds of things: local attractions like our park which has real pigs in it, local events like the hanging basket competition, and forthcoming shows at the Civic like the history of the Eurovision Song Contest (told in an hour with over twenty costume changes).

Jenny and I like having a laugh over the leaflets, pretending we're going to go to really naff stuff and sometimes actually being tempted to go to some of the better things. We once saw a leaflet for a chocolate-tasting competition and went along. That was a good afternoon. All we had to do was guess which bar we were eating. Jenny and I kept pretending we'd got it wrong so we could have more chocolate.

I rushed to the loo and put on my Bella clothes. When I got to leaflet heaven Jenny was already looking through the leaflets.

'To be honest, I think you're better off without Remi,' she announced.

'Why didn't you say anything before?' I asked, surprised.

'Didn't want to spoil your fun. And I could be wrong, but he seems really vain.'

'Really?' I said, as I quickly tried to remember all the conversations I'd had with him.

'Yeah. He's always fiddling with his hair and he wears a different earring every day.'

'You're right,' I agreed, the truth dawning, 'I think he's obsessed with appearances.

Today he said my t-shirt was weird!'

'How could he?' said Jenny, looking admiringly at my tight pink t-shirt. Of course she didn't know Remi had seen me in an Anna t-shirt. Still, she was right about Remi.

'When I went to the football match, all he said to me was, "You look good" and "Nice to see you out of uniform".'

'He probably wanted to check your clothes were cool before he asked you on a proper date.'

'What a cheek!' I was going off him by the second.

'My thoughts exactly.'

Having trashed Remi, we got on with looking at the leaflets. It felt good to take my mind off boy trouble.

Suddenly Jenny went all serious, 'This sounds like us,' she said, peering at the leaflet. Then she thrust it at me: 'Let's do it!'

It took me a while to take it all in. The leaflet was all in silver and black. In the middle in shiny letters was the word 'TALENT' and underneath, 'Have you got it?' The small print explained that a talent competition would be held at the Civic at the end of the month. I immediately imagined the stage where I'd seen the Irish dance, full of kids singing, playing recorders and juggling beanbags. The winners from each area would appear on a new television talent competition. You could do any kind of act, either alone, in pairs or in groups.

It sounded exciting but I wasn't sure I should go in for it. 'We've got *A Bug's Life* coming up – do you think we'll have time for this as well?'

'Of course! *A Bug's Life* rehearsals are only once a week and it's not on for ages! This talent competition is on in a couple of weeks. That's masses of time to rehearse.'

I felt my spirits slowly lift. It would be good to do something like this. It was performing, like at Spotlight. It might take my mind off all the problems of being Anna and Bella. And of course Bella loves performing . . .

'Maybe,' I said tentatively. Jenny took that

as a yes and hugged me. We spent the rest of the afternoon planning what we would do. First we decided we'd tell jokes but then we could only think of three so we ditched that idea. Then we thought we'd do a dance routine but Jenny's got no sense of rhythm so we let that idea go too.

Finally I had a brainwave, 'Let's do a comedy dance routine. No one else will think of that! All the other girls will just want to wiggle around to the latest hits.'

'Did I ever tell you you're a genius?' asked Jenny, deadpan.

'No, but you may.'

'You're a genius.'

The day was looking up, and we went back to Dad's to rehearse straight away. We tried out lots of music but we went for ballet in the end. When we tried pop routines we just looked like we were trying to be slick and not managing it, but with the ballet we could be as clumsy as we liked and it worked. Well, it made us laugh, anyway.

We spent the rest of the afternoon

rehearsing but then it was time for me to go to Mum's.

Jenny asked me the dreaded question, 'Can I come to your mum's tomorrow? We can do some more rehearsing . . .'

She's asked me before and of course I've always had to make up an excuse rather than tell her the real reason and the excuses have got more and more ridiculous. This time it was: 'Er – no, I don't think that's a good idea because she's taken up meditating and she needs absolute silence in the house.'

'Yes, but she doesn't meditate all day, does she?'

'Most of it, yes.'

'So she meditates as well as having an unfriendly dog, a cleaning obsession, tidying the house for the estate agent and being a part-time witch?' Jenny was throwing all the excuses I'd given her back at me.

'Yes, she's quite a busy person.'

'Busy being nuts, if you ask me.'

The tense moment between us lifted and we started joking again, but I still felt sad inside. I so wanted to tell Jenny about Anna but I was too afraid. Afraid she'd be angry, let down and, most scary of all, not want to be my friend any more.

NINE

On Sunday I went to Olly's. Even though I couldn't do anything about Anna and Bella, I might be able to do something about Olly. In any case, I wanted to know why he had left the Centre so hurriedly and hadn't waited for me to 'get rid of' my 'boyfriend'.

Before I turned into Olly's street I reminded myself to stop wiggling my hips and I started thinking Anna thoughts about sewing and soldiers instead of Bella thoughts about clothes and boys.

Olly wasn't painting in the window but he did open the front door.

'Not painting today?'

'Everything's wet,' he said grimly.

'Can we go for a walk?' I asked humbly.

'Yup,' he said, and grabbed his jacket, which is an old army one, of course.

As we fell into step going down the road I felt really sad that what I was about to say would change our relationship for ever, but I knew I had to say it. We couldn't go on as we were, that's for sure. I went straight to the point.

'I'm sorry about what happened at the Centre,' I started.

'Yeah, it was pretty grim,' he said soberly.

'Yes, sorry about that,' I repeated. 'If it's any consolation, the other boy's gone off me.'

'The one I saw you with?'

'No, another one.'

'*Another* one?' said Olly incredulously. He must think when it came to boys I was greedy.

'Anyway, you don't need to worry about the other boys.'

'I'm not.'

'Because what happened made me realise something about you.'

'I'm not as fit as them?'

'No! Nothing like that.' I paused. I was getting to the hard bit. 'It's about going up to the park.'

'Well, we're not ever going to do that, are we?' he said quickly.

'No,' I said, relieved to be honest with him, for once. 'But I've only just realised that. I always thought I wasn't quite ready for the park. I thought that I was too young and I just needed to wait a bit, even if it meant making you wait a bit too.'

'You've certainly done that,' he said as we turned the corner back into his street. I realised we'd walked right round the block.

'Yes, sorry about that,' I said yet again.

'So have you finally decided you don't fancy me?' he said, looking hurt.

'No! It's not like that. I've realised that you're my *friend*, not my *boyfriend*. You've always been my friend, really. It's just we called it boyfriend when we were in primary school.'

He was silent for a moment or two and then he said, 'Yeah, you're right.' I felt so relieved I could have hugged him but that might have confused us both again. 'I realised that at the Centre. That's why I went off. I wasn't really interested in who you were with, or not with, or nearly with, or once with.'

I laughed at how daft he made me sound. We'd arrived back at his house. Then he said something only boys say.

'I've had enough of talking about all this emotional stuff.'

'Me too.' (I pretended I agreed to make him feel comfortable when really I could talk about it all day.)

'Do you want to come in for some crisps?'

'Not today, but soon.'

'OK. My paint should be dry now.'

'Yeah. See ya.'

'See ya.'

He plodded up the steps to his house.

I was amazed by the talk we'd just had. I didn't think boys were able to talk about their feelings like that. It made me like Olly even more – as a friend – that he could share all that stuff with me. As I walked home along the sleepy Sunday streets I felt something new, but nice. I felt that Anna had grown up a bit. She'd stopped running away from romantic stuff and faced it head on. Maybe Anna was getting a bit more like Bella.

For a few moments I felt all warm inside. That made me realise I'd been feeling cold and confused for ages.

And the chilly spell wasn't over yet.

When I got back to my mum's I was ready for a rest. As soon as I walked in I realised I wasn't going to have one. To my amazement, Eve was in the kitchen, talking to Mum. I thought she was so angry with me she'd never come round again. Actually, Mum was talking to Eve, boring her to death about patchwork.

'You always have light and dark fabrics,

to represent the light and dark side of life,' droned Mum, holding up some dreary black corduroy and some lovely slippy shiny stuff. 'I'm going to make these into a giant quilt, as soon as I get my new workshop.'

'When will that be?' asked Eve, doing her best to sound interested.

'Just a few weeks now.'

As soon as I came in Eve turned round and leapt out of her chair, 'Hi!' she said, unnaturally bright.

'Hi,' I said back, trying to sound positive. I wasn't ready for another emotional roller-coaster. Last time I'd seen Eve she'd been all judgemental about Remi; I didn't want another dose of that.

Eve suggested going up to my room which made me suspect that she was going to put me on trial again. We left Mum to her light and dark patchwork. Once we were in my room and the door was shut we both started up.

'Sorry,' we said in unison. That actually made us laugh a bit.

'You go first,' said Eve, but not crossly. I took a deep breath. I was going to be emotionally exhausted by teatime.

'Sorry about all that boy stuff. I've sorted it out now.'

'Well, I'm sorry I interfered and told tales. It's none of my business, really.'

'Course it is!' I protested. 'You're Anna's best friend,' I said. As soon as I said it I realised it sounded weird. So did Eve.

'That's an odd way of putting it,' she said suspiciously.

'I mean *my* best friend,' I said, trying to put Jenny out of my mind. Eve fiddled with the edge of my bedspread which is patchwork, of course.

'So it's all OK now?' she asked.

'Yup. I've just been to see Olly and we're going to be friends.'

'And you'll go out with the football boy.'

'No, that's over too.'

'Oh,' she said, and I think she probably wanted to know more but didn't dare ask and I didn't feel like telling her any more. I wanted to move on. I felt I'd really begun to sort my life out, well Anna's anyway, and I was ready to settle into some nice relaxed Sunday afternoon sewing. Perhaps it was punishment for daring to think I was out of trouble, because I was back into it within seconds. Eve put her hand in her pocket and got out a crumpled piece of paper. It wasn't so crumpled that I didn't recognise it. I began to feel quite chilly again.

'I've found out about something I think will cheer us up, get us over this tricky time.' She brandished a leaflet at me, 'There's a talent competition at the Civic!'

'Really?' I said, trying to sound interested and surprised.

'Let's go in for it!'

I tried to look cheery but how could I when my heart was sinking so low I thought it might fall out of my trousers.

TEN

I tried everything. I said I was too shy. Eve said it would help me get over my shyness. I said it was on a Dad day. She said I could swap like I had before. I said I had a sore throat. She gave me a hot lemon drink. Of course what I didn't tell her was that I was already going in for the talent competition with my other best friend Jenny.

Understandably, she got quite shirty. 'I thought it would be a nice thing to do together after all that horrible Olly stuff, but if you don't want to . . .'

'It's not that I don't want to . . .'

'Well, what is it then?'

I was cornered. All I could do was to ask for more time. 'I need some time to think about it.'

'How long?'

'I don't know.'

'Five minutes?'

'No! Longer.'

'Ten minutes?'

'No! I need to ask Dad about it. I'll tell you when I'm back here – on Tuesday.'

Eve was being very pushy – especially for her. Maybe she was feeling insecure about all the weird stuff that had been going on recently. I think she realised she was being pushy because she started backtracking. 'But if you really don't want to . . .'

'I do! I just need to sort a few things out.'

'OK.' Phew. I finally had some peace. 'Like what?' she asked. Did I say I had some peace?

'It doesn't matter what! I'll tell you if I can do it on Tuesday.'

*

My, oh, my. The talent competition didn't feel like much fun any more. I had 48 hours to decide what to do. Of course one option was to tell Eve that I was already going in for it with someone else. That didn't seem fair – on Eve, or on Anna. Why should Bella get to go in for the competition when Anna couldn't? After all, they're two different people so why couldn't they both enter the competition?

Maybe it was possible. But was I kidding myself, and everyone else? Could I really rehearse two acts, and perform them on the same day? I started to think it through, working out when and where I'd change. I must admit it began to feel quite exciting. And terrifying. But at least it was me that was taking on all the difficult stuff and not my friends. I owed it to Eve and Jenny to let them go in for the competition with Anna *and* Bella. They didn't deserve to be mucked around by my silly split personality.

On Tuesday Eve came round straight after school and I told her the good news:

that I had sorted everything out and I would go in for the talent competition with her. In a flash, tense, tetchy Eve disappeared and sweet, enthusiastic Eve returned.

'Let's do something Irish!'

'I'm not wearing black tights,' I said.

'Have I even mentioned the word "black" or "tight"?' said Eve innocently.

'No, but there's always a danger you will.'

'Actually, you're right, because I think you should wear "black", "tight" . . .' She slowed down, building up the tension. I wiggled my fingers, ready to tickle her nearly to death. 'Trousers!' she said, leaping away from my tickling tentacles. '*I* can dance,' she said, showing she could by doing a few steps, 'while you sing that sad ballad!'

I had to drop the tickling strategy then because it was actually a really good idea. Eve's got this CD of sad Irish songs which we play when we want to feel sad about things like world poverty and not going to the same secondary school. There's a song about a lost seal on it and we always sing along to it at the top of our voices.

Bella would have been fine singing on her own, but Anna was worried about it. 'I'm not that good at singing.'

'It doesn't have to be good, it just has to be sad.'

I bought that argument for the time being and got on with rehearsing.

Luckily I was so busy I didn't have time to dwell too much on what I was doing. Whenever I was at Mum's I rehearsed with Eve; whenever I was at Dad's I rehearsed with Jenny.

In between I had *A Bug's Life* rehearsals. Rich was going all arty now. We didn't just rehearse the play we had 'character' sessions, where we talked about what our characters thought of each other. Jimmy and I had to do a session on Flick and Princess Atta. While Rich got everyone else going on scenery painting, Jimmy and I sat by the radiator at the other end of the hall. Jimmy picked bits of flaking paint off the radiator while we waited.

'All right?' he said vaguely, not looking me in the eye.

'Yeah,' I said back, and then: 'Thanks for the other day.'

'That's OK,' he said. 'Did it work?'

'Sort of,' I said. I didn't want to go into it all. 'I'm not seeing either of them now.'

'Right,' he said and smiled.

'By the way,' I said quietly, 'can you sort of not mention it to Jenny? I feel a bit stupid, juggling boys like that.'

'OK,' he said.

Luckily I didn't have to talk about all that boy stuff any more because Rich came back. He sat down and ran his hands through his hair. I think he was just checking it was still there. 'Right, then, Bella, so what does Princess Atta think about Flick?'

'Um – I think at first she doesn't notice him because she's worried about everything else.'

'Good, yes, and what does Flick think

130

of Atta, Jimmy?' Jimmy kept picking at the paint.

'Er – he thinks she's great but she's too posh for him and she's so busy she'll never notice him unless he does something amazing to get her attention, sort of . . .'
I was impressed but I didn't let it show. I didn't think Jimmy would have been aware of all that. Rich was impressed too.

'Great, Jimmy. And of course we in the audience are aware that they like each other right from the start . . .'

Just then there was a scream from the other end of the hall. Tamara had accidentally plonked her foot in a pot of paint . . .

The rehearsing frenzy went on for the next couple of weeks. Jenny and I leapt around at Dad's, sometimes bruising ourselves with pratfalls and failed attempts at the splits. At Mum's Eve and I were so moved by the tragedy of our act that we could hardly get through to the end.

When the acts were rehearsed nearly to death we turned our thoughts to costume and make-up. Unfortunately Mum had done the same and offered to make us 'something suitable', which of course it wouldn't be. Eve quickly said she was wearing her usual Irish dance costume, and I foolishly said I wanted to wear something I 'hadn't had much wear out of'. I didn't say this because it was true, I said it because I knew it would get Mum off the track of making us something yukky.

Mum loves the idea of 'getting wear' out of things. When most people make a bad buy they take it back. Not Mum. Mum thinks you should wear things which were actually a bad buy until they're worn out, and then use them for painting, and when they're too worn for that, use them as dusters, and when they're too worn even for that, recycle them.

I had something in mind. Last year I went through a very odd phase of wanting to look like a witch. Maybe it was because deep down I felt evil to be two people at once. I bought a witch's dress at a boot sale: it was black, full length, with long, wide sleeves. It only cost one pound which was a bargain considering the material, which was thick velvet.

That's another annoying habit of Mum's that I've inherited. She never sees clothes for what they are, she thinks of them in terms of what they could become. So if, say, a dress doesn't suit you, it could always be cut up and re-sewn to make shorts. A coat can become a handbag, a skirt can become a scarf, a shirt can become a shirt, but smaller and dyed a different colour.

The 'cut and sew' gene had given me the idea that the black velvet dress could make a matching jacket and purse, but luckily I hadn't mentioned it to Mum so the dress was still intact at the back of my wardrobe. I took it out and showed it to Eve, she agreed with me that it was perfect. With black pumps, black ribbons in my hair and a touch of black eyeliner I would look suitably tragic.

The clothes for Bella's act with Jenny were

a bit trickier. I suggested something like a pierrot.

'What's that when it's at home?' asked Jenny quizzically.

'It's a sort of French clown,' I told her, 'they wear white and have masks.'

She liked that idea, and I particularly liked it because the mask would help disguise the fact that I was in two acts. As soon as we'd decided to go for white clothes Jenny announced that she didn't have any white clothes. Nor did I, but I had already worked out where I could get some: the nutty clothes shop. As the clothes were arranged on rails according to colour I could head straight for the white one and choose.

This time the cat was asleep in the window. As the bell rang and I walked in it opened a lazy eye, only to shut it again. The shop was empty. I made straight for the white clothes rail. I found a skimpy little jumper and baggy cotton trousers for me, and a huge t-shirt and cut-off jeans for Jenny. All the clothes were white, but different shades, if that's possible. I guess it must be because when I've gone to buy paint with Dad we've had to choose from Bright White, Apple White and White White.

I was just adding up how much I'd spent when the owner came in. She was wearing the same long black coatdress and she was carrying a big green potted plant.

'How much do I owe you?' I asked, showing her the pile of clothes.

'Do you actually want to buy them?' she asked as she put the pot plant down. I was a bit taken aback. I thought buying was what you did in shops.

'I need them for a talent competition,' I blurted out. I hadn't meant to tell her that.

'Then why don't you rent them? Much cheaper.' I hadn't thought of that.

'OK,' I said. 'How much will that be?'

She gave the clothes a cursory look and muttered, 'Two quid. For a week.'

She was busy polishing the plant's leaves so I left the money on the table, picked up the clothes and made for the door.

'Bye,' she called, 'and good luck.'

'Bye,' I mumbled as I left. I decided she was weird, but in a nice sort of way.

ELEVEN

Even though I was really busy with the talent competition rehearsals, it didn't stop me worrying about *A Bug's Life*. The day when I had to kiss Jimmy was looming. Trouble was, there wasn't much I could do to prepare. I tried kissing my mirror but it made me laugh because I looked like a fish. I tried kissing my teddy but he couldn't really kiss me back. I looked up 'stage kiss' on the internet, and even though there were six million entries, none of them actually told you how to do it.

I decided I'd just have to improvise. Rich was always encouraging us to do that. As

I walked to the hall I realised that I wasn't really nervous about kissing Jimmy, in fact I was quite looking forward to it. I was just worried about getting it wrong and everyone laughing at me.

I needn't have worried about that. When I walked into the hall Rich and Jimmy were the only people there. I wondered if the others were all hiding, ready to leap out, point and laugh when we got to the kiss, but Rich explained that he thought it best if we rehearsed this scene on our own first time. I was so relieved I could have kissed him, but I didn't. Kissing Jimmy would be enough.

Then Rich, like a fairy godfather, offered to wave my fears away entirely. 'You know, you don't have to do the kiss if you don't want to. It's in the script but we don't have to do it.'

'It's OK, we'll do it,' said Jimmy confidently.

'Yup, it's OK,' I said, not wanting to be chicken.

There was no way out now. We rehearsed

the scene and when we got to the kiss bit I sort of went into a trance. Bit weedy, I know, but at least I didn't scream and run out of the room. Instead, I shut my eyes and felt Jimmy give me a soft, gentle kiss on the mouth.

Well if I'd known it was going to be as easy and nice as that, I wouldn't have worried. It was over and I had survived. Now all I had to do was do it again in front of the rest of the group and then in front of masses of parents and friends. Easy. The only thing I had to work on was the colour of my face afterwards. It was beetroot with blushing, but perhaps the more I practised the less I'd blush.

I shot a secret glance at Jimmy to see if he looked as flustered as I felt. He had his nose buried in his script, so I couldn't tell.

Rehearsals for *A Bug's Life* were a nice break from the trauma of the talent competition. As the day grew nearer I had to work out how I was going to organise myself so no one found out I'd entered the competition twice.

This was the naughtiest thing I had ever done and I felt a bit ill even thinking about it. Feeling ill gave me the idea that I could actually pretend to be ill to get out of the whole competition but I decided that didn't solve anything because Eve and Jenny were both really looking forward to it and I'd be letting them down.

I'd entered the competition as Anna with Eve and Bella with Jenny; I'd got two different addresses, so that was OK. I had to put the same date of birth, but it was entirely plausible that two girls with the same birthday could enter the competition. Maybe they'd think we were twins. Then I worried that twins wouldn't have different addresses, but I worked out that they would if their parents had divorced and each kept one twin. That made me wish that Anna and Bella were twins and could actually be in two places at the same time. Unfortunately they weren't, and I had to make do with my quick change and acting skills.

I worked out how to handle the day.

Both acts involved dance, so we were in the same section. This was both good and bad. Good, because I couldn't win two prizes which would be a nightmare when they were presented; bad, because it meant there wasn't much time between the two acts.

I got round that by telling Eve I had to rush off straight after to a patchwork exhibition with my mum – one of the few advantages of having a split personality is that you can use the same excuse twice to different people who are never going to meet. I got round Jenny by telling her it would make me too nervous to get there early, so I'd meet her just before we went on. Then I said that I had to rush off to my dad's tomato show straight afterwards. It was kind of true: Dad was putting his tomatoes into a show, it was just a week later. That was the bit I left out. The plan meant that I wouldn't be there to pick up a prize if either act won, but Eve or Jenny could pick up the prize for me, like they do at the Oscars. Except I wouldn't be filming on the other side of the country, I'd be in the loo stuffing tissues down my bra.

The day of the competition finally came. Even though I was terrified I wanted to get on with it. I didn't know if what I was feeling was stage fright or 'life fright', a kind of fear of what I was doing with my life.

After a final rehearse of my song, I got into my long black dress at Mum's. The only suitable coat I had to wear over it was my school mac, so I reckon I looked pretty weird, but then I guess wearing a velvet evening dress on a Saturday morning would look pretty weird anyway, so the mac wouldn't make much difference.

I packed my white pierrot clothes in the bottom of my bag, with a mag on top of them in case Eve glanced inside. I said goodbye to Mum, who wished me luck. She wanted to come and watch but I said I was too nervous, which was true but of course it wasn't just because I was performing, it was because I was performing twice as two different people with two best friends who would kill me if they found out. I'm not surprised I was nervous.

When I got to the Civic it looked totally different from the evening of the Irish dance show. There were no weary programme sellers; instead the foyer was filled with nervous competitors and their even more nervous parents. Mothers were fiddling with daughters' hair, fathers were giving sons pep talks, younger brothers and sisters were getting in the way but no one had time to tell them to stop.

Eve was waiting for me as she said she would, by the box office. She looked all organised and compact. She was in her Irish dance uniform and I felt like there was a little circle of calm all around her. I realised then that Eve had been in these competition conditions loads of times, and it didn't faze her.

I was just beginning to calm down when the swing door that led to the auditorium swung open and a fierce looking old woman poked her head out. She had pointy glasses and her hair in a tight bun; she was carrying a clipboard.

'Registration! Form a queue and sign in.'

Registration! No one said anything about registration. Jenny wasn't here, she wasn't coming until later and that had been my idea! I couldn't get her to come along now because she'd see me as Anna. How could I register our act? Maybe they'd let us perform without registering? I couldn't risk it. I'd have to register the act for both of us now.

While I was thinking all this I lined up with Eve. She was humming happily to herself, oblivious to the storm going on in my head. The queue in front of us was quite long. I suddenly had an idea and acted on it.

'Can you register for us? I need the loo.' Of course I did need the loo, but not for the usual reasons.

'Course. Are you OK?' asked Eve.

'Yeah. Just need the loo,' which wasn't a total lie. I tried not to draw attention to myself by rushing to the loo. I did a smooth, fast walk, reckoning as I went that if I changed really quickly I could register as Bella, change back into Anna and be ready to perform with Eve.

I pushed open the door to the loo, ready to rush into the cubicle. There was a queue! Why are there never enough girls' loos? The boys only take seconds but the girls take hours. Maybe they're all changing identity, like me. I didn't have time to dwell on that nutty idea, because I had to act fast. I rushed to the front of the queue, grimaced at the girl whose turn was next and mumbled, 'Sorry!' as I clutched my stomach and barged into the free cubicle. I felt bad about what I'd done but told myself I wouldn't have minded if someone did that to me.

I changed as quickly and quietly as I could: off came the big, black dress and on went the white stuff. Off came the black pumps, on went the white trainers. I even stuffed my tissues down my top, although no one there would know that Bella was a 32C and Anna a 32A, but it made me feel better. Finally I put on my mask, then I opened the door a fraction to check that the queue had moved on and no one in it now would recognise me from before and wonder why I'd gone in as one person and come out as another. Phew. The queue had moved on, there was a new queue of nervous girls.

I went back out into the foyer, trying not to look like I was rushing. Eve was at the front of the queue! I queued up behind her, signed for Jenny and me, then did the whole quick change all over again, including tissues.

By the time we got to the green-room where we waited our turn I was exhausted. It was a shabby room with worn out sofas and armchairs, half covered with Indian-patterned throws. In one corner was an old sink with mugs draining on the sideboard and a little fridge with tea and coffee stuff crammed on top of it.

The sparse room was brightened by other performers waiting to do their act. Most of them were moving around, either pacing nervously or practising their steps. A few muttered the lyrics of songs under their breath. I took my lead from Eve. She sat quietly on a chair and stared into the middle distance, not really focusing on anything, it seemed.

I did the same, and when I did, I realised what she was doing: she was focusing on the act, but internally, rather than let all her energy spill out and get wasted.

As acts were called one by one, they rushed to the door, giggling and fussing. Soon we were the only ones left in the room, but we still sat quietly, not talking much. Then our names were called over the tannoy and we got up, really calmly, walked out of the dressing room, down the corridor, through a heavy door and into the backstage area. We handed our tape to the technician and walked calmly towards the brightly-lit stage.

'Good luck,' whispered Eve as we left the safe shadows of the backstage.

'And you,' I whispered back. We walked out onto the stage. There were a few little bursts of applause, as if the other competitors who had done their acts and were dotted around the theatre didn't know how supportive they should be. The judges were sitting a few rows back from the front. We couldn't really see them because the lights shining at us were dazzling.

Just as I got used to the brightness the music began. Eve began to dance, and her confident steps calmed my beating heart. I took a deep breath and started to sing. Once we'd started it seemed like a tiny hop to the end. Before I knew it we'd finished and were taking a bow. Now it was over our focused calm left us and we jabbered at each other.

'I was so nervous I thought I was going to wet myself!' shrieked Eve.

'No! I only calmed down because you looked calm . . .' I admitted, clutching her arm.

'But I was only calm because *you* looked calm!' We both laughed, enjoying the relief. At that moment I forgot all about doing the other act with Jenny and all the fibbing I had ahead of me. I soon remembered, though weirdly enough, it was Eve who reminded me.

'It's two already,' she said, 'don't you have a date with a patchwork?'

The fun was over then but I tried to keep smiling for Eve. I pretended that I needed to go to the loo.

'Again?' she asked. I was cornered. I hadn't planned on the loo visit to change for registration, so I'd already used the loo as a cover for changing once. Thank goodness I hadn't actually NEEDED to go to the loo as well. That would have made this the third time. I quickly thought of a new excuse.

'I must be nervous.' It was a terrible excuse and she immediately saw through it.

'But we've done the act now.'

'I know,' I said, desperately trying to come up with something, 'but now I'm nervous about the result.'

'Don't worry about it,' she said cheerily.

'There's nothing we can do about that now. I'll ring you the minute they announce it.'

'OK,' I said and dived into the loo to change AGAIN. Then I set off to find Jenny.

I think I must have taken a wrong turn out of the toilets. I walked along a concrete corridor which I thought led back to the foyer, but it turned a corner, and then another, and by then I had no idea where I was going.

I was relieved when a door at the end of the corridor swung open and a man walked towards me. I could ask him the way. I smiled and he smiled back, but then his smile dropped and mine did too.

It was Rich from Spotlight. He'd recognised me because I'd forgotten to put my mask on.

'Hi,' I said, as if it were the most normal place in the world to meet, 'what are you doing here?'

'I'm a judge,' he said, 'and what are you doing here – apart from cheating?'

TWELVE

The game was up. I don't know why I'm calling it a game because games are meant to be fun and this was no fun at all. I felt like turning round and running back down the corridor but I knew I'd get lost again and then Rich would find me again and the whole horrible cycle would probably go on for ever.

'You know you're only allowed to enter the competition once?' he said, trying to look me in the eye but he couldn't because I was looking at the floor.

'I have,' I said desperately. 'I'm just wearing these clothes for fun. And I called myself Anna for the act for fun too.' My excuses were going downhill at an alarming speed.

'Don't make it worse by fibbing. I've seen your name on the register as Bella *and* Anna.'

'No, no, Anna is my twin sister,' I said. Well I didn't really say it, I nodded and mumbled it, blinking a lot because I knew I was going to cry. He took my arm and led me back through the door he'd come through. I felt like a filmstar caught shop-lifting. He walked slightly ahead of me, as if he wanted to get this horrible episode over with. I did too, but I wanted to go backwards, to before it ever started, and not let it begin. He didn't say anything, and I didn't either; I just looked down as my tears fell onto my shoes.

I wasn't so upset that I couldn't think of the implications of what had happened. My Anna/Bella awareness was always with me, even at moments of great distress, like this one.

'Please don't tell anyone about this,' I asked tearfully.

'I have to tell the judges. You'll be disqualified.'

'I know, but don't tell anyone at Spotlight.' To my surprise, I was thinking of Jimmy. For some reason I didn't want him to know how bad I'd been.

'OK, but whatever made you do this, you have to sort it out.'

'Yeah,' I said vaguely.

'We can have a chat about it, if you like, at Spotlight. Try and work it through.'

I could think of nothing worse, but I mumbled, 'Maybe,' to be polite.

Rich knew his way around the place, and after a few swing doors and turns in the corridor, we suddenly arrived in the foyer. It was like splashing in a pool at the end of a long twisty flume, but of course not nearly as much fun.

The foyer felt smart and carpeted compared to the bare concrete of the backstage area. The same stuff was going on as before:

people practising and fussing. I didn't look round much because I didn't want anyone to see I was crying, but without even lifting my head, I could see Eve's little black shoes. She was chatting to some other dancers who'd arrived. Sadly, she wasn't involved enough in the chat not to notice me. She broke away from them and came towards me.

I looked up at her, knowing there was no way I could explain this away, especially as I could also spot, looming like a monstrous shadow, my totally unmonstrous other best friend Jenny. They both reached me at the same time.

'Anna!' said Eve.

'Bella!' said Jenny, at exactly the same time. Then they both looked at each other and the look said, 'Who are *you*?'

'I've got to get back to the auditorium,' said Rich gently, letting go of my arm. 'I'll tell them you've withdrawn.' He went back through the doors to the backstage.

'What's Rich doing here?' asked Jenny.

'Judging,' I muttered.

'Who's Rich?' asked Eve, looking worried. 'What did he mean about withdrawing?'

'What about our act?' quizzed Jenny.

'What act?' Eve demanded, hurt spreading over her face.

I didn't answer. I just cried and cried and cried. They each put a hand on my arm.

'Anna?' said Eve again.

'Bella?' said Jenny again. Then Jenny got a bit assertive with Eve. 'Excuse me, but are you sure you've got the right person? This is my friend Bella.'

'No it isn't. She's my friend Anna,' answered Eve. Finally the moment came when I couldn't hold it in any more.

'I'm both your friends!' I wailed. 'I'm Anna with Eve and Bella with Jenny. I'm two completely different people!' I stood there sobbing. I could feel everyone in the foyer staring at me. I suddenly had an intense need to get away from the situation. I felt like a cat caught in the glare of bright headlights. I was frozen, but then I did what a cat would do.

I ran.

I ran straight past Eve and Jenny. Through the foyer. Out of the Civic and along the street. I thought they might run after me, but they didn't. I'm not sure I'd run after a two-faced, two-timing friend either.

I ran right to the end of the street and turned the corner. I stopped then, because there was no point running any more, and because, despite the tears and the running, I'd noticed something unusual among the boring silver cars parked along the street: a black limo. Although I really couldn't be less interested in cars, and I can't tell a Mini from a Mercedes, I immediately recognised it as the one I saw outside Spotlight the day I got Jimmy to pretend to be my boyfriend.

I hung back a bit then, I don't know why. I wanted to see what happened next, because a man in a suit got out from the driver's seat, walked round to the back and opened the door on the pavement side. I've seen enough TV clips of royalty and celebrities arriving at red carpets to know that this was a chauffeur, but I'd never actually seen one in real life, and certainly never expected to see one outside the Civic in my little town.

As if this weren't weird enough, I then saw a boy get out of the back of the car. He was dressed in a sharp suit. That's another thing you never see where I live: suits. The boys at school wear blazers, and one of them came back from a funeral once wearing a baggy black suit, but I've never seen a suit in a non-death situation.

I soon stopped being shocked by the suit, though, because I realised I knew the person inside the suit. It was Jimmy. Jimmy in a sharp suit! Where had he got it from and why was he wearing it? Maybe he was going in for the competition. Perhaps he was doing an act as a smart type, or maybe he reckoned if he dressed like Mr Successful they'd make him the winner.

I was intrigued to know what he was up to but I didn't want to stop and ask him because I was a mess: half comedy clown and half blubbing wreck. I looked around for a place to escape. No such luck, the street was all offices, shut on a Saturday.

Jimmy started to walk towards me. I decided the only thing to do was to front the situation. I sniffed, wiped my eyes and strolled forward, as if it was completely normal to be dressed as a clown with a tear-stained face on a Saturday afternoon. Jimmy was near me now and I could see the horror in his face. Was it horror at him seeing me, or me seeing him? Whichever it was, or both, it soon disappeared. I'm sure both of us were thankful for our acting classes, because we could both pretend.

We were near each other now and we both did the same thing: looked away and muttered, 'Hi,' at the same time.

I was past him now. I couldn't have been more relieved. I felt like the whole hopeless situation was behind me, even though I knew it had really only just begun.

THIRTEEN

I changed in the nutty shop before I went back to Mum's. I wondered why I was bothering. I'd told my friends the truth so why didn't I now tell Mum and Dad? I winced at the thought. It still felt too tricky. Anna was how Mum wanted me, Bella was how Dad wanted me. I couldn't imagine that changing.

When I got to Mum's I went straight into the kitchen and slumped down on top of a whole load of material on a chair. Mum didn't even comment or maybe she didn't notice because she was threading a needle, which takes her about a day because her eyes are so bad.

'How did you get on?' she asked.

'We didn't win,' I answered.

'Well you know what they say . . .'

'No.'

'It's not the winning it's the taking part.'

I felt like saying: 'What do they say about being disqualified?' but that would be saying too much and would open up a can of Anna/Bella worms.

'Got anything unhealthy to eat?' I groaned instead.

'Of course,' she said. 'Lardy cake. It's swirly cake with fat in between.' She broke off a bit and I stuffed it in my mouth and chomped on it. It was actually *too* unhealthy, even for me.

'Have you got an apple?'

'Yup,' she said, chucking me one. I chomped on the apple instead. Mum seemed very busy and preoccupied. I looked over to see what she was doing now, she was trying to find her keys. Nothing odd about that, she does that whenever she wants to go out, although she doesn't always end up going out because she can't always find them.

There was something odd about Mum, though, and it took me a while to work out what it was. When I realised I felt really shocked. She didn't have bits of cotton thread all over her! I hadn't ever seen her like that before.

'What are you doing?' I asked.

'Looking for my keys,' she muttered wearily.

'No, I mean, where are you going?'

'Nowhere, if I can't find them.'

I peered at her again. Why on earth would she have smartened up? A suspicion dawned.

'You're not meeting a man, are you?' That stopped her in her tracks.

'Of course not!' she said, looking behind the blender. I relaxed then. The idea of Mum going out with someone else was just as bad as the idea of Dad going out with someone else, if not worse.

In a flash I thought of all the things I wouldn't be able to do with her if she had a boyfriend: cuddle on the sofa watching telly, sit on the end of her bed in the morning and chat, go looking for starfish and crabs on our holiday at the seaside.

If she got a new boyfriend they'd probably lie on the beach smooching and drinking wine; he'd try and be my friend by reading teen mags and talking to me about 'boy trouble'; then they'd probably go and have a baby which would mean they'd never talk to me again, except to ask me to babysit. I shuddered at the thought of all this. As I came out of my reverie I realised I was running ahead of myself, and Mum, in my daydreams; but they were still pretty scary, even if they were only daydreams at the moment. That I preferred to think of them instead of what had just happened with Jenny and Eve shows you just how totally awful I was feeling.

I came dazedly back to reality and started looking for the keys. Then I became aware that I wasn't just sitting on material. There was something firmer underneath. Like the princess with the pea, I reached under all the soft stuff and brought out Mum's keys. I handed them to her with a sigh; she ignored it and grabbed they keys.

'Actually, I am meeting a man,' she said, and then she looked at the clock and left, without another word of explanation. I sat there and started panicking about stepdads again. Before I'd had time to really get going, Mum came back in the door.

'Did he stand you up?' I asked.

'Who?'

'The man.'

'No!' she said, a bit irritated. 'I can't find my purse.' She rummaged around a bit and found it in the fruit bowl. 'He's not that kind of man,' she then added. 'He's the Leader of the Council.'

'Oh,' I said, relieved. 'Do we owe them money again?'

'No!' said Mum, affronted, as if she were never late paying her bills, which was extremely far from the truth. 'I'll be back at six.'

'So why are you meeting the Leader of the Council?'

'He's threatening to take away my workshop,' she said darkly, as she checked her purse for money.

'The one for your patchwork?'

'Of course. They've got a new plan to use the building for a school,' she said, distracted, as she slammed her purse shut and whisked out of the door.

Poor Mum. Just when she thinks something good is on the horizon someone has to build a horrible school in front of it. I decided to ring her on the mobile to wish her luck, but once I'd dialled I heard it ringing, she had left it behind. I don't know why she has a mobile, it isn't a mobile at all, because it's always on top of the fridge.

I didn't do much while Mum was out. I stayed in the kitchen and actually found myself fiddling with bits of Mum's material. I chose lots of bright materials I thought might go together but they just looked a mess. A mess like me, I thought. Like me, the pieces that work fine on their own don't work at all when you put them together. I still couldn't imagine who I'd be if I were just one person. I couldn't kill off Anna to be Bella, and I couldn't kill off Bella to be Anna.

While I was fiddling with the patchwork pieces there was a knock at the door. It made me jump. Usually I'm pleased to hear a knock because it might be Eve. Now I was frightened to hear a knock because it might be Eve. I got up and crept to the edge of the window, like a gangster or a goodie in an action film. I stood with my back to the wall and looked out of the window sideways, so I could see without being seen.

It was Eve! Probably come to shout and scream and tell me she hated me for ever. I shrank back into the corner of the room and held my breath. I didn't go and open the door because I couldn't face seeing her. She knocked again. I held my breath even more, if that's possible. She knocked one more time, really loudly, then waited for a while, then walked away.

I came out of my corner and breathed many sighs of relief. I knew I couldn't avoid Eve for ever but at least I'd managed to avoid her for now.

Mum didn't have much luck at her meeting with the Council Leader, but she came back really fired up.

'It's a scandal,' she said, frantically cutting out hexagons. 'They promised me a workshop at the Grove Centre, and now they're trying to go back on the whole deal. Well, I'll show them. A protest! That's what's needed. There's plenty of places a school could go . . .'

'Absolutely,' I said, impressed but a bit exhausted by Mum's new drive and ambition.

As the days wore on, I wished some of that drive and ambition had rubbed off on me. I had never felt *less* driven or ambitious.

I had never felt more hopeless or useless. I moped about on Sunday, dreading Monday morning. I would have to face Jenny at school. I imagined all the things she might say to me, all her anger and disappointment. I didn't want to be on the receiving end of all that.

I went to school as late as I possibly could, without actually getting a late mark. Jenny was already sitting down, so I picked a desk as far away from her as possible. I worked really hard, with my nose in my books, to avoid her stare. As soon as the lesson finished I rushed out and into the loos. I seemed to spend a lot of my life in loos. Maybe I should have picked a different place to hide because within seconds of locking myself in I heard Jenny's voice.

'Bella?' she said, knocking on the door.

'Go away!' I shrieked hysterically. 'Leave me alone!' There was a pause. A long pause. Perhaps she was deciding what to accuse me of first: lying, cheating, betrayal, immaturity, neurosis or just being an idiot. I listened out for her accusations even though I didn't want to hear them.

None came. Nothing. Only her footsteps retreating back out of the loos. I was relieved but not relaxed. She was probably waiting until she could have a real go at me, without a bolted door between us.

I had thought it was a good idea to avoid Jenny but it actually made me feel worse. I now dreaded the confrontation even more. On Monday night at Dad's I took drastic action: I pretended I had an ultra-bad stomach ache. Although I'd never pretended to be ill before, I'd heard people at school say that this was the best illness to feign because there's nothing to prove you have or haven't got a stomach ache: no temperature, no rash, and no medicine except bed rest.

I put myself to bed. Dad was really nice which made me feel worse – not ill, but guilty. He brought me a hot-water bottle and some gardening magazines. I'm not really interested in gardening but they were the only ones he had.

I made sure I seemed just as bad the next morning, so I didn't have to go into school. But by lunchtime I was going crazy just slumped in bed with only an article on growing better beans to distract me. So I told Dad I felt a bit better and would go over to Mum's. He was surprisingly OK with my plan, particularly as he said he had to go out. Again? How many gardening classes can a person do in a week?

When I got to Mum's the kitchen was completely unrecognisable, and that was because I could actually see it. She had tidied all the material into neat piles, the floor had been cleaned; in the middle of the table were her bag, her keys and her mobile.

'What are you doing here?' she asked in surprise. 'What happened to school?'

'I was feeling sick,' I said. 'Now I just feel like I'm dreaming. What's got into you?'

'Organisation,' she announced. 'I've

decided to let it into my life.'

'And how long is it going to stay?' I asked cheekily.

'At least until I get that workshop,' said Mum decisively. 'I'm off to a protest at the council offices this afternoon, with all the other workshop-wanters. We're meeting at the Shopping Centre first. Coming? It might take your mind off feeling sick.'

'It might,' I agreed. It was actually really nice to see Mum like this, especially as I was so miserable. I decided to go with her. It might at least distract me from my Anna/Bella problems for a while. I put on a really old tie-dye t-shirt and some scummy jeans so I'd look a bit like a poor kid whose mum desperately needed a place to work. I was even ready to put on some pale make-up so I looked *really* ill, in case people wondered why I wasn't in school. But when I checked the mirror I saw I looked pale and ill and awful anyway. Guilt and raw emotion are definitely no good for your skin.

The other people who'd all been promised workshops were dead odd. There was a woman who made paper jewellery, a man who made lavender pillows and another bloke who made clogs. Mum had got them all fired up and they were ready to riot. At the meeting today, the fate of the Grove Centre – and my bedroom – would be decided.

When we got to the council offices it was hard not to feel intimidated. They were so clean and quiet and modern. It felt like we were a circus troupe at the Houses of Parliament. The doorman showed us into the council chamber. It had huge long windows with thick draped curtains, a big table with men and women in suits all round it. At one end were a few chairs for ordinary people like us.

I recognised the Leader of the Council from photos I'd seen in the paper. I glanced round the table. Sitting next to him was someone I would never have guessed would be there, even if you asked me 20 questions, or 50 questions, or 100 questions.

Dad wasn't at gardening class at all. He was right here.

FOURTEEN

Dad saw me just as I saw him, which was pretty awful because I didn't have time to prepare my face. If I *had* had time I could have prepared a slightly surprised face, or a calm and cool one. The face he got to see was a totally amazed one: my eyebrows shot up my forehead and my mouth dropped open in an unflattering gawp.

Dad's reaction was much more controlled. He managed a toothless smile – not because he hasn't got any teeth, because he has – he just didn't show them off. He added just a hint of a raised eyebrow to suggest that he wasn't expecting to see me there.

Needless to say, Mum noticed him too, and her reaction was as childish as his was mature. Perhaps this was because he had all the power, the power to make decisions that would affect her life, and she was sitting on the fringes, waiting to hear what would happen. It was too close to their marriage for comfort.

'What's he doing here?' she hissed theatrically at me.

'No idea,' I said.

'Like I believe that . . .' she muttered, revealing that she's totally in touch with that 'inner child' she's always droning on about.

'Well you should believe it because it's true.' I replied forcefully.

Then the meeting began. As soon as the Leader did the introductions it became clear that Dad was representing the architects who were going to convert the Grove Centre into a school. So he was the enemy! One of the dastardly developers who were going to stop Mum getting her patchwork workshop.

He sat there, looking all professional, as he consulted the plans, plans he had been working on for weeks instead of spending time with me.

Mum was fidgeting next to me, clearly agitated by the way her future was being decided by a load of people in suits. Dad meanwhile appeared totally unruffled. I felt completely sandwiched between the two of them, but not in a happy sandwich way, like cheese and tomato or ham and cucumber; it was an unhappy sandwich like jam and cabbage. In supporting Mum I was going against Dad, and it would be exactly the same if I supported Dad; I'd be going against Mum.

The meeting was between the council and the workshop people but I felt the real argument was going on between Mum and Dad, even though they weren't actually talking to each other. I couldn't ignore the argument, like I tried to do when we were still a family, because it was also an argument between Anna and Bella. I felt as if I were being pulled so hard in two directions that I was going to snap.

The words of the meeting went over my head. I sat rigid and deaf, locked into the impossibility of my situation. Slowly I became aware that the meeting had ended, the council people were picking up papers and shuffling them into a pile. Mum and her gang were turning round and muttering grumpily at each other. I clicked out of my frozen state in time to realise that the meeting had gone against them: the Grove Centre would definitely be converted into a school. I felt totally split, as if one side of me was warm and the other frozen. It was just like toasting my front by the campfire while a chill wind whistled around my back.

The councillors and everyone round the table left the room, and we followed, moaning as we went. I half-listened as we plodded down the ornate staircase and out into the early evening air.

'Why couldn't they have put the school on the other site?' said the clogmaker.

'What a waste of time,' said the paper jeweller.

'We'll never get our workshops now,' moaned the lavender pillow man.

We congregated outside the council to do a bit more moaning. Mum was busy joining in and didn't see Dad come out of the council offices and walk straight towards us. I flinched as if I was about to be mown down. I felt like I was in the middle of a shoot-out in a Western.

Dad just wellied in. He didn't bother to keep his voice down or move away from the rest of the group. I thought he'd be on about the workshops. In all the drama I'd completely forgotten about the obvious source of tension.

'What's the point of me spending all this money on her when you dress her in rags?' he barked.

Mum launched a counter-attack: 'Excuse me, but a) *I* don't dress her, b) What you spend on clothes when she's with you has nothing to do with what she wears when she's with me and c) This is a totally inappropriate—'

'Don't do all that inappropriate at me, Eileen – Bella told me . . .'

'Bella? Since when has she been Bella?' queried Mum.

'Since last year, of course. Don't tell me you're still calling her that stupid baby Anna name? I never liked it.'

The crafty people tried to keep talking amongst themselves as if they weren't listening but I knew they were because they kept making those big wide eyes at each other as if to say: 'Listen to that!' Mum and Dad were still at it.

'Look at her!' he hissed. 'She looks as if she's been kitted out at a boot sale.'

'She has!' said Mum proudly. 'And she looks a lot better than she did in that inappropriate get-up I saw her in at your place . . .'

'Inappropriate for what, exactly?' asked Dad coolly.

'Inappropriate for her age! She's only a—'

'Don't say "little girl", Eileen. She's nearly 13 years old, almost a—'

'Don't say "woman", George, because she's not ready for all that—'

'You mean *you're* not ready—'

'SHUT UP BOTH OF YOU!!!' someone screamed. Everyone turned and stared: it was me that was screaming. 'You're tearing me apart and it's not fair! You've split me into two people because you won't let me be myself!'

'Anna,' said Mum, starting to cry.

'Bella . . .' said Dad, moving towards me.

'Yes, I am Anna *and* Bella,' I went on, 'I'm Anna with you, Mum, because you want me to be a little girl and never grow up, and I wear old clothes and eat bacon and do my sewing with Eve . . .' I was really ranting now. I couldn't stop. 'And I'm Bella with you, Dad, and I wear skimpy clothes and eat lettuce and go to Spotlight with Jenny . . .'

'Who's Jenny?' asked Mum.

'She's my *other* best friend. I haven't told

179

you about her because you don't really want to know. I was trying to protect you from who I am. But I can't any more, and I won't. This is me, you can take it or leave it.'

Then I just stood there sobbing.

'Oh well! Here's the bus,' said the paper jeweller, and then he and the other craft people moved off towards the bus stop. I couldn't actually hear a bus but then I was crying so loudly I probably drowned it out. Or they were just being polite and moving away from our rowing. I didn't really care which it was.

It was very quiet. Mum and Dad both put an arm around me. I think Dad was crying as well as Mum and me.

My, oh, my. I felt completely exhausted.

'Time to go home,' said Mum.

'Which home?' I said miserably.

'Whichever one you want,' said Mum.

'Well it's your day . . .'

'Forget about whose day it is,' said Mum. 'Where would you like to go?'

'I don't know.'

'Why don't we have a cup of tea, and then decide,' said Dad.

'Good idea,' said Mum. If I hadn't been so upset I think I'd have fainted at them actually agreeing with each other.

There was a little café round the corner. It was nearly closing time and it was empty, apart from us. The owner was putting away all the food. It didn't matter, we only wanted a drink. Dad had coffee, Mum had tea, and I had a problem.

I was being Anna and Bella at the same time. Anna would want juice, Bella would want coke, so what should I have? Juice and coke mixed wouldn't be very nice. I decided to forget about Anna and Bella and just have what I felt like. It took a moment or two decide but then I knew, it was hot chocolate.

We all sipped our drinks in silence and then Dad piped up, 'Seems to me,' said Dad, 'that you've been trying to please me and your mum. Maybe it's time to please yourself.'

'I agree,' said Mum, instantly beating her record by agreeing with Dad twice in a day. 'So why don't you start by choosing where you want to stay tonight.'

I took a deep breath. I looked at their tired faces as I tried to decide. I couldn't – not yet, but I came up with an idea of my own.

'I'll toss a coin. Heads for Mum's, tails for Dad's.' Dad provided the coin and I tossed it. It was heads, so I was going to Mum's, which is where I would have gone anyway on a Tuesday, but it felt better going because fate had decided rather than our rigid rules.

I was so tired when I got back to Mum's, I had an early night – so early it was almost a late night from the day before. Mum told me the next day I had missed another visit from Eve. Just as well, I thought.

After sleeping for so long I felt a bit better. Now Mum and Dad, and Jenny and Eve had found out the truth, and however they felt about it at least they *knew*. Rich sort of knew too, which I guess was helpful – although maybe not that helpful because now what name would he give me on the cast list in the *Bug's Life* programme? Anyway, I didn't think I needed to tell Olly yet, and I really wasn't bothered about Mr 'Vain' Remi. So what was the problem?

I worked out what the problem was while I was walking to Spotlight on Friday. I was still avoiding Jenny, but luckily (for me, not for her) she had been off sick for real the last two days, so I was fairly sure it was safe to go to rehearsals.

I was daydreaming about Jimmy: wondering if I'd ever see him in that slick suit again. Then I realised that I felt like telling Jimmy about Anna and Bella, but I wasn't quite sure why. And then I got into a big debate about it in my head. It was Anna v. Bella, big time.

'You don't need to tell him,' said Anna, *'he's only a boy in* Bug's Life.*'*

'Only a boy?' said Bella. *'He's pretended to be your boyfriend AND you've kissed him.'*

'Only in rehearsals,' said Anna.

'Yes, but it was nice,' said Bella.

Anna: 'What's that got to do with it?'

Bella: 'I think you like him.'

Anna: 'That doesn't mean I've got to tell him.'

Bella: 'If you don't, you'll have to always be Bella with him.'

Anna: ' I suppose it's not very honest either.'

Bella: 'So be honest and tell him.'

Anna: 'OK, but what if he doesn't like Anna?

Bella: 'He's already met Anna, when he was pretending to be your boyfriend.'

Anna: 'Yeah, but I wasn't just Anna then, I was sort of Anna AND Bella.'

Bella: 'Yeah, and that felt good, didn't it.'

I blinked, like I'd been sleeping and someone had prodded me awake.

Anna: 'Yeah, it did.'

And then came another voice in my head: 'Just shut up a minute you two!'

Who was that? It was someone I'd heard before – yes, it was the girl who'd chosen hot chocolate in the café with Mum and Dad! It was someone new, someone who wasn't Anna OR Bella, but the best of them both.

I decided that this was someone I would really like to be.

By the time I'd got to the Spotlight hall I'd decided to definitely tell Jimmy – but I didn't want to tell him there and then. I had a plan, and I decided to suggest it to him during the break, but before I had the chance to go over and talk to him, HE came over and talked to me . . .

'You know the other day when I was wearing all that smart gear . . .'

'Outside the Civic?' I asked, even though I knew that's what he meant.

'Yeah,' he said. 'It was only cos I was going in for that talent competition.'

'So what was your act?'

'Kind of smooth singer . . .'

'Right. How did you get on?'

'I won.'

'Oh. Congratulations.'

'Ta.'

I wasn't going to tell him about Jenny, Eve and me getting disqualified. Not yet, anyway.

I launched into my plan, 'I need to talk to you about something. Could you meet me tomorrow?'

'OK.'

'I'll meet you at the Shopping Centre, by the fountain.'

'No holding hands this time?' he asked, almost smiling.

'Promise,' I said.

'Pity,' he said.

'Really?' I checked, and I couldn't hide my smile.

'Only joking,' he said.

I forced my smile to grow wider and pretended to laugh. Funny kind of joke.

He was waiting at the fountain when I got there, even though I was early too. I wore Bella clothes because it was technically a Dad Saturday, even though he had bravely said I could choose to spend it with whoever I wanted. Choosing at the moment felt way too scary, especially with my head in such a whirl, and I didn't want to upset Dad when he was acting so nice. He was actually trying to *listen* to me for a change. So how come I had nothing much to say? Why did it seem so tempting and easy to fall back into the old routine?

And why did I think that everything would be easier once Jimmy knew the truth?

Jimmy was used to seeing me as Bella, but I did my hair like Anna because he'd seen me as Anna too and hadn't seemed to mind. I couldn't believe that I didn't feel weird mixing my selves up like this, but it felt OK. This was a good sign. Maybe I was really beginning to change.

Jimmy was wearing old jeans and unlaced trainers, as usual. I explained that I'd suggested meeting there because we both knew it, but that I was going to take him somewhere else. I led the way, past all the bright shops in the Centre, out into the dull afternoon, across the car park and into the smaller, shabbier streets.

We were soon at the nutty clothes shop. The dog *and* the cat were asleep in the window and the fairy lights were now coloured. I marched into the shop and called out: 'Hi,' loudly and as casually as if I were at home. In a way, I was. I often felt more at home there than I did in my other two homes.

'Hi there,' called the shop owner back. 'I'm mixing fertilizer. Can't stop.'

'That's OK. We're fine here,' I called back. Jimmy looked a bit confused. I launched into my little speech. 'Right – well – there's something odd about me.' Jimmy stared at me. He looked a bit frightened. 'I'm not always how I seem.'

'What d' you mean?' he asked, understandably a bit confused.

'Wait there,' I said, pointing at where he already was. 'I'll show you.'

I slipped behind the Japanese screen and took the Anna clothes out of my bag. I changed out of my Bella clothes and put on Anna's soft velveteen joggers and an old baggy t-shirt. I left my hair in Anna bunches but pulled out the Bella tissues from my bra and used them to wipe the Bella make-up off my face. I looked in the mirror at Anna and took a big deep breath.

This was a big moment. Jimmy, who only knew Bella, was about to meet Anna. He was going to find out about the real me. The real 'mes', I should say, as there are two of us. Three if you counted the hot chocolate girl, who I hoped was still about somewhere inside.

I strode out into the centre of the shop, trying to be brave. Jimmy looked me up and down. He didn't actually look that surprised.

'I've seen you like that before, that first time at the Civic,' he said.

'Yeah. And when you pretended to be my boyfriend. Didn't you think it was weird?'

'Yeah, kind of. I sort of thought you were in a different mood.'

'I was a different person. Anna,' I said. 'This is how I am at my mum's. When I'm at my dad's I'm called Bella and I'm like I am at Spotlight.'

'What d'you do that for?' he said.

'Because I feel like two different people,' I said, being honest.

'That's stupid. You can't be two people.'

'But I am! Bella's all confident and Anna's quite shy; Bella's adventurous and Anna's cautious, Bella likes lettuce and Anna likes bacon.'

'OK, but you can't go on being two people.'

'I know I can't, but I can't seem to stop myself doing it either.'

'Course you can. It has to stop, right now. Because it's stupid, just stupid.' Before I had a chance to answer him he kind of lunged towards the door and left. As I watched him go I thought about what I'd just done and felt sick. I realised how stupid I'd been. The guy I'd kissed at Spotlight, that was just a character, a part being played – not Jimmy. Somehow, for some weird reason, I thought he could make me feel whole.

Fat chance. I guessed this was something Anna/Bella would have to do by herself.

I mean – by *my* self.

There she was again! That new person. If only she would stop feeling so scared and stick around for a while.

FIFTEEN

Next week was half-term so I had time to play around. I mixed up Anna and Bella a bit to see how it felt. I wore heels at Mum's and ate a salad; I didn't hoover at Dad's and read a book without a shiny cover. I was starting to feel better about the new me until I remembered Jenny and Eve and how angry with me they must still be. *That* got me thinking about Jimmy and how angry *I* was with HIM for not seeming to understand my situation.

I couldn't avoid Jimmy because it was Spotlight on Friday and it wasn't a good idea to miss rehearsals so near to the *Bug's Life* show – even if that meant facing up to Jenny at last. Would she be professional enough to let us play our parts on stage as they were written, or would she burst on stage in our first scene and shriek that I was the biggest liar ever and she hated my guts? Rich was always encouraging us to improvise, but I wasn't sure that would go down too well.

I walked to the hall slowly, hoping that if I went slowly enough I would never arrive. But despite my attempts at a snail's pace I *did* arrive, and as soon as I got through the door I wished I hadn't.

In the little entrance hall I was confronted with a terrifying sight: Eve and Jenny sitting together, both with their arms crossed. They had ganged up on me! Now I was in for it!

I knew I couldn't get past them so I stopped in my tracks and crossed my arms too. Maybe it would make me look tough. But they took me by surprise by uncrossing their arms. I left mine crossed, just in case.

Then they did something really weird. They stood up, came over to me and both put their arms round me. What on earth was going on?

'I've missed you,' said Eve.

'Me too,' said Jenny.

I stared, my mouth flapping open and shut like a goldfish with bad indigestion. 'I – I've had some things to sort out.'

'Well you look pretty sorted to me,' said Jenny, pulling away and looking me up and down. I was wearing old jeans and heels, a bit of an Anna/Bella mix.

'Don't you think my jeans are a bit old?' I said to Jenny.

'No.'

'And I like your shoes,' said Eve, pointing to the heels. 'They look really good on you.'

This was crazy! Were they changing as much as me? 'Sorry about the competition,' I said to them both.

'Doesn't matter,' said Jenny. 'It was good in a way. At least we found out what was going on.'

Eve nodded. 'The reason for all your weird behaviour and quick exits. If we hadn't, you might have wound up torn in half!'

'And that would have been well messy,' Jenny agreed with a smile.

I found I couldn't smile back. 'Yeah, but after all that time we spent practising, you didn't even get to perform our act.'

'Yes I did. Eve persuaded me that I should. On my own.' She shrugged. 'I didn't win, but I got loads of applause.'

I looked at Eve. I was amazed. And then I was worried. 'Have you two been seeing a lot of each other?' What I really meant was 'Are you two best friends now, without me?' but that was too scary to say out loud.

'No!' they both exclaimed, and then Jenny went on. 'We just exchanged phone numbers – to see if we could help sort things out.'

'You mean sort ME out.'

'Only you can sort yourself out,' said Jenny wisely, 'but maybe we can help.'

'Yuk,' I said teasing. 'Which mag did you read that in?'

195

'Can't remember,' joked Jenny. 'It's in most of them most weeks.'

I couldn't believe we were joking again. Eve reminded us that we'd be late for rehearsals so Jenny and I went in, after Eve and I had made an arrangement to sew the next time I was at Mum's.

I went into the hall in a state of shock. It was a good shock though. My two best friends knew about each other and didn't hate each other. They seemed to still like me, too.

Jenny went off to help Rich sort out the costumes. Jimmy was sweeping the stage. No one else was around. I wished I'd asked Jenny to stick with me so I could avoid talking to Jimmy. He was wearing a scraggy old football kit and even more battered trainers than usual. He barely glanced at me when I came in so I decided he was still being mean. I ignored him and got to work, carrying lights out of the storeroom.

I was in the storeroom, lifting a spotlight out of the corner, when I became aware of a shadow falling on me. I turned round and saw Jimmy hovering in the doorway, darkening the space. He leant on the door, trying to look casual, but also getting in my way.

'Sorry about the other day,' he said quietly.

'Did we do something?' I said, pretending I didn't remember. I wanted to forget the whole business.

'You know, in that shop.'

'Oh yeah,' I said, 'I wish I hadn't told you.'

'No, I'm glad you did. I just got a bit freaked out by what you said.'

'Well I guess it *is* weird.' How could I ever have imagined he would understand?

'Bella – I mean, Anna – I mean . . .'

'Look, don't worry about it. In fact forget it,' I said.

'Listen, we're having a bit of a bash at my place next week. If you want to come along . . .'

'You don't have to invite me because you feel sorry for me.'

'I'm not! Look, I'll give you the address,' he said as he reached into his pocket.

'It's OK. I wouldn't want to freak you out again,' I said. 'I'll see you around.'

He looked a bit deflated, like a helium balloon days after a party, but didn't try to talk me round.

I felt really mean saying no, but what was the point in going to his house when I was still angry with him for not accepting Anna and Bella. My parents and my girlfriends had, so why couldn't he?

I couldn't work out what was going on any more; some days I felt almost whole, other days I was totally in bits. After my miserable encounter with Jimmy at Spotlight – coming so soon after the high of finding Jenny and Eve still liked me – I felt pretty much in bits. When I got to Mum's on Saturday I went straight upstairs and flung myself on the bed. I planned to read all afternoon in an attempt to forget all my identity crises.

But Mum came in. She was holding something wrapped in tissue paper. 'I've made you something,' she said, and opened up the paper. 'It's patchwork, but I think you'll like it.'

It was a shoulder bag; she handed it to me. It was made out of lovely warm materials: velvet and brushed cotton and wool, with flowers and roses and hearts on. I recognised them all, they were scraps from dresses I'd had when I was little, they were all 'Anna' materials and they reminded me of the little girl I was at Mum's. I felt like crying.

'Don't worry, this isn't all of it,' she said.

'But I really like it.'

'You'll like this even more.' She took the bag and turned it inside out. The lining was now the outside and it was completely different. Some of the pieces were jeans, embroidered or faded or torn, some of them were shiny, some silky, some with sequins and some made of leather and plastic. They all reminded me of 'teenage' Bella.

'Did you cut these bits out of my clothes at Dad's?' I asked, bemused.

'No! I just remembered the kind of clothes you were wearing when I came round that time. Then I bought some scraps.' I turned the bag inside out again. I really, really liked it.

'You can choose which way to have it, depending how you feel,' said Mum.

'You mean depending whether I'm Anna or Bella,' I said. It felt weird, talking about that to Mum.

'Whatever. You know, Anna, I know it'll sound soppy, but I want to tell you something I read in one of my sewing books, "Life's a patchwork: you can't always choose the pieces, but you can choose how you put them together".'

'Yuk. That *is* soppy.'

'I know, but it's true isn't it? Light and dark, rough and smooth, soft and hard – it's a weird mixture . . .'

'But it looks great!' I said as I tried the bag out on my shoulder.

SIXTEEN

'I thought we could go out this afternoon,' said Dad on Saturday morning, a week later.

'What for?' I asked suspiciously.

'I want you to meet someone.'

So I was right to be suspicious because there it was: the moment I'd been dreading all these years. I pretended I didn't know what he meant. 'It's not some kid you think I'll get on with?'

'No. It's a woman. Someone I met at my gardening class. She's called Rose.' So much information, all in one sentence. I felt overloaded. Dad went over to one of his tomato plants and felt the soil with his fingertips. It came clear to me now: he didn't just love plants, he loved another gardener.

'Rose. Funny name for a gardener.'

'It's a lucky co-incidence,' said Dad, smiling.

'So is she moving in, then?' I said, a bit tartly.

'No!' said Dad, shocked, 'well not yet, anyway. We're going out this afternoon, and I thought it would be nice if you came along.'

'How would that be nice?' I knew I was being foul but I couldn't stop myself.

Dad gave me a look. '*I* thought it would be nice. I know it might not be nice for *Bella*, but I'm not so sure about this new, budding daughter who seems to be outgrowing her.'

Despite the gardening references that made me feel a bit better. Even so I still couldn't stop myself being cheeky, 'Where are we going? To some old black and white film with subtitles?'

'No. We're going to visit a garden.'

'I'd rather go to the film.'

'It's Open Garden week, and there's an amazing garden on the other side of town we'd like to visit.'

'Can't you visit it on your own and take me out for some cake afterwards?'

'No, we can't. Rose and I think it would be much better if we did something together rather than sit and talk.'

Rose and I la-de-da. 'Why don't we go bowling together instead?'

'You can't hear yourself talk at bowling.'

'Oh all right then, as long as it doesn't take too long.'

'You'll like her.'

'How do you know?'

I was pretty sure I wouldn't like her. In fact, I decided I'd make sure I didn't. Rose was a stupid name, for a start. Gardening was a stupid hobby, and it was totally mean to tear my dad away from me when I'm only 12 and trying to get over an identity crisis. I made sure Dad knew I still wasn't keen on the idea by hardly talking and not eating my lunch. He looked quite concerned. I knew I was being mean but I couldn't stop myself. I used my fork to skewer a piece of tomato.

Dad took a deep breath, and said, 'I've invited her for you, you know.'

'I don't need a girlfriend.'

'No, I've invited her because I wanted to show you that I'm scared.'

'Of her?'

'No.'

'Of me?'

'No. Of the situation. Of my life moving on.'

I stopped skewering. This was worth listening to properly.

'I think maybe I'm a bit like you,' said Dad. 'You're finding it hard to move on from being Anna and Bella. And I'm finding it hard moving on from being Divorced Dad. It doesn't make any difference that I'm about a century older than you. The feelings are the same.'

Luckily, this intense moment was under-cut by a ring at the door. The bell plays the theme from *Countdown* and it always makes us laugh.

I let Dad go and open the door, even though I was now dead curious to find out what she looked like.

I didn't need to find out what she looked like because I already knew, in our hall stood the owner of the nutty clothes shop.

She was wearing the long black coat-dress, like she did the first time I saw her. She smiled at me. 'Hi there,' she said, like she always did.

'You're the nutty shop owner,' I blurted back.

'I'm a shop owner, but I didn't know I was nutty,' she said.

'No, the shop's nutty.'

She smiled, 'I suppose it is, really.'

I couldn't work it all out. 'How did you know I was me?' I asked incoherently.

'I didn't. How did you know I was me?' she asked back.

'Do you two know each other?' asked Dad, looking on, more than a bit confused.

'Yes,' we said together.

'Bella comes into my shop,' said Rose.

'Did you know she was my daughter?' asked Dad.

'I had no idea.'

'And I had no idea she was your secret girlfriend,' I added.

'No more secrets,' Dad declared. 'From now on, let's keep everything out in the open.'

'Except your scrawny tomato plants,' I said wisely, and was glad to see that Rose smiled at that.

'Shall we get going?' said Dad.

I got in the back and they got in the front. It felt really weird, like having two parents, which of course I'd always had, but not in the same car. It didn't feel nearly as bad as I thought it would. I think it helped that I already kind of knew Rose so it wasn't like Dad was just introducing me to her. We talked more about how strange it was that Dad had met her at gardening class and I'd met her in her shop. I teased Dad a bit about how he'd suddenly got so interested in gardening.

Dad and Rose didn't talk much. I noticed Dad occasionally glanced over to her and then put his hand on her knee. Even now, I kind of wished it was Mum sitting there instead of Rose, but I knew that would never happen again. All that stuff belonged to another life. Now a new one was beginning.

On the other side of the park the houses get bigger. It's like everything's on a bigger scale, and the houses are whiter and the light is brighter. The houses are detached, and they have big gardens, and two or three cars parked outside in the gravelly drives.

We soon turned into a drive that was even more gravelly than the others: the stones were bigger and there were more of them. At the entrance to the drive were two big black wrought iron gates, newly painted. Tied to one of them was a small, discreet, laminated notice saying 'Open Garden 10–6 today' with pink and red roses beautifully drawn around the letters as decoration.

The drive was so long you couldn't even see the house at the end of it. We drove slowly through the deep gravel. The drive turned a corner and suddenly, in front of us, was a huge, amazing house, like a small palace. There were roses growing all round the front door, which was shiny and black.

At the front there was a mini car park, with a few flashy, highly-polished cars in front of the house which I guessed must belong to the owners, and lots of smaller, shabbier ones like ours, which I guessed must belong to the visitors.

'This is a bit of a disappointment,' said Dad, joking, as he got out of the car.

'Just because it's big doesn't mean it's beautiful,' said Rose, putting her hand in his. I pretended to do up my shoelaces so I wouldn't have to look. Didn't work really because I wasn't wearing shoes with laces.

At the side of the house there was a sign in the shape of a hand with a finger pointing towards the back of the house. Written on the hand were the words: 'Garden this way'.

I began to wonder if we'd ever actually see any people. It was all a bit quiet and creepy.

As we turned the corner at the side of the house I immediately realised this wasn't a ghost house, or garden. At the back was a bright and huge expanse of flowers, which I recognised as roses. They're about the only flower I know because they prick and smell so good. Staring, wondering and sniffing at the roses were all kinds of people: old, hunched people with sticks who could barely bend down far enough to get a whiff of rose; serious gardening types in long green wellies who were peering at the flowers and taking notes; a couple of mums, with loads of little children, who were trying to look at the flowers but had to keep turning away to referee fights.

'Wow!' said Rose, 'Roses, my favourite.'

'Mine too,' said Dad, looking at her all soppily. I suddenly felt cold with fear. An icy shiver shot down my spine. Perhaps they were actually going to do a wet soppy kiss, right there in the rose garden, in front of dozens of people, and worst of all, in front of me. I turned away. Rose was nice, and all that, but I didn't actually have to watch her and Dad practically making a baby in front of my eyes. Dad was moving on, all right. In fact, he was moving on so fast I felt like it was time for me to push off. I walked away while they weren't looking. It was easy for Dad to move on because he had Rose. Anna and Bella didn't have a boyfriend between them.

Luckily I saw a gap in the tall, thick hedge that surrounded the rose garden. I made straight for it. There was more garden on the other side, stretching as far as I could see. I could just about work out that it was divided into sections: there was a green bushy bit that looked like herbs; a bit with canes and nets that looked like fruit and vegetables; a large, perfect lawn that looked as if it had been cut with nail scissors.

I didn't dare walk on the lawn even though it didn't say you couldn't. I skirted round the edge of it and made my way to the other side of the house where there was a walled-off section of garden. I could hear laughter and chatter and tinkling glasses from the other side of the walls. I headed towards it because I'm far more interested in people than plants.

When I got close to the walled garden I saw another little sign with roses round it. This one said 'Private'. As soon as I saw it I knew I had to ignore it, however Anna or Bella might feel about that. I popped my head round the side of the entrance to the walled garden. No one noticed. They were all too busy being posh.

It was like looking into an exotic bird house when you've only ever seen pigeons. The people in the walled garden were all shiny and colourful. The women wore silky dresses and lots of make-up; the men were mainly in suits and open-necked shirts. I decided this must be the owner's party, although there was no knowing who the owners actually were.

Suddenly, the throng of posh people

parted politely and I saw a couple of boys push their way through them. There was a little one, and he was hanging onto the big one like a mussel on a rock. The big one was holding a huge red strawberry up in the air, out of the little one's reach. The little one, who had dark curly hair and a determined look on his face, was shouting, 'It's mine, James, mine!'

The little one leapt up at the strawberry. The big one reached higher with it, and then, with a huge gulp, chucked it in his mouth and swallowed it in one. It was only then that I really looked at the big one. I had been distracted by the little one and the strawberry. How could I not have noticed that the big one was Jimmy?

Yes, Jimmy from Spotlight, my once pretend boyfriend. But he was looking smart again, in the suit I saw him in on the day of the talent competition. What was he doing here and why was the little one calling him James?

While the little one complained to a tall

elegant lady who could have been his mum, Jimmy crossed his arms and listened. Then he said, 'It's not true, Mother, he's already eaten a couple of dozen,' in an incredibly posh accent. I was amazed, and without really thinking about what I was doing, I marched into the walled garden. I went straight up to him and tapped him on the back like a teacher ticking off a school kid. He spun round.

'Bella,' he said, still talking posh. 'I thought you said you couldn't come?'

I frowned. 'What do you mean?'

'I asked you to this party – don't you remember?' Once he'd said that, I did, but the person who'd asked me at Spotlight was so different from the one standing in front of me now, I didn't connect them up.

'So *this* is where you live?'

'Er – yes, it is,' he said, all embarrassed. 'And that's my mother,' he said, pointing to the tall elegant lady. 'And that's my brother,' he pointed to the little boy who was still stuffing himself with strawberries.

'And is that your suit?' I asked, nodding at his clothes.

'Yes,' he said, fiddling with one of the buttons.

'So when you wore it to the talent competition it wasn't a costume.'

'No. I performed as myself. For a change.'

'Why didn't you tell me all this?'

'I wanted to, but I bottled out.'

'Fair enough, but then why were you so mean to me in the nutty clothes shop?'

'Because I know how painful it is to be two people. But if I couldn't stop myself from doing it, how could I stop you?'

The reality of what he was saying slowly sunk in, 'So are you always posh James when you're here, and rough Jimmy when you're at Spotlight?'

'That's right.'

'Why on earth do you do that?'

'I'm embarrassed by all this ...' he gestured vaguely to the huge house and garden.

'Some people would show off about it.'

214

'I don't. I want to be like everyone else.'

'So you've ended up with two personalities. Like me.'

'Yes, like you.'

'But we do it for different reasons.'

'Yes, and I've had enough of it. It gets complicated when you know there's someone you want to get close to,' he said, looking me shyly in the eye. 'And I've been trying to stop doing it. But I've got so used to being Jimmy and James, it's hard to change.'

'Yes, it is,' I agreed.

'And when I saw how confused and upset your split-personalities were making you, I realised how crazy it is.'

'Yes, it is,' I said again, and I really meant it.

The party was spinning on around us, with not a care about our life-changing conversation. They probably thought we were talking about computer games, or our favourite chewing gum.

'Shall we stop doing it, together?' he said.

It sounded so simple, the way he said it. 'It'll be easier together,' I agreed.

'OK,' he said, and almost as soon as he'd said it, he frowned, 'but I don't know whether to call myself James or Jimmy.'

'You can call yourself Jamie,' I said confidently.

He smiled at that.

'Jamie. OK. What's your name going to be?'

'Annabella,' I said. There was no hesitation, no doubt, none at all. 'My name is Annabella.'

It was finally time for the *Bug's Life* performances, and even though I was nervous, I was excited too. Jenny and I looked out from the wings at the audience. Jenny spotted Eve first and I had to stop her sticking her hand out and waving. Eve and Jenny get on really well and sometimes we go out together – but they don't get on as well with each other as I get on with both of them! They're still both my best friends and that's fine by all of us.

Eve came to see the show with Olly. I couldn't quite see in the glare of the spotlight, but I think I saw them holding hands . . . Dad and Rose DID hold hands, but I didn't mind and Mum didn't even seem to notice. She was standing next to the soundboard, chatting to Rich . . .

The show went really well, even the kiss with Jamie at the end. Fact was, we'd done quite a lot of practice by then, and not just in rehearsals . . . At the end, when we were taking our bow, Jamie and I were holding hands and it felt like the audience were applauding us, not just because we'd acted well in the play, but because we'd sorted ourselves out. Maybe the people in the audience who knew us were doing just that.

After the show, in the middle of our dusty church hall, I introduced Rose to Mum. And you know what? The ground didn't open up. No one was struck down, and no one got their hair pulled. All that happened was that Rose noticed my shoulder bag.

'I like your bag,' she said.

I smiled at Mum as I took it off my shoulder. Then I showed Rose how I turn it inside out, depending on how I feel.

'I made it from bits and pieces that didn't work on their own,' said Mum.

'But they're wonderful together,' I said. And just saying it made *me* feel wonderful. Those patchwork pieces reminded me of me, Annabella, together at last.